Keeping
track??

HIGH PRAISE

"Randisi always turns out a traditional Western with plenty of gunplay and interesting characters"

—*Roundup*

"Each of Randisi's novels is better than its entertaining predecessor."

—*Booklist*

"Everybody seems to be looking for the next Louis L'Amour. To me, they need look no further than Randisi."

—Jake Foster, Author of *Three Rode South*

"Randisi knows his stuff and brings it to life."

—*Preview Magazine*

"Randisi has a definite ability to construct a believable plot around his characters."

—*Booklist*

NO CHOICE

Lancaster was walking back to his hotel when the first shot came. The bullet went wide as he dropped into a crouch and turned. There was a man standing about twenty feet behind him, legs spread, gun in hand.

"That you, Lancaster?" a voice called. "I can't see ya. Come closer."

Hector Adams, the ex-deputy.

"Come on, Lancaster. Step into the light."

"Deputy, you don't want to do—"

"Before you came to town I had a job," Hector Adams said. "After you got here, I got fired. I ain't stupid, ya know."

"You could've fooled me. This seems real stupid to me. Trying to shoot me in the back while you're drunk."

"Front, back, I don't care. Let's do it."

Hector fired again, missed by a wide margin. Lancaster heard glass break.

"Hector—"

He fired again. Came close enough for Lancaster to flinch. Lancaster drew his gun. . . .

Robert J. Randisi

GALLOWS

LEISURE BOOKS NEW YORK CITY

A LEISURE BOOK®

October 2009

Published by

Dorchester Publishing Co., Inc.
200 Madison Avenue
New York, NY 10016

ISBN 10: 0-8439-6178-3
ISBN 13: 978-0-8439-6178-2
E-ISBN: 978-1-4285-0744-9

GALLOWS

Chapter One

Lancaster spotted the house and felt lucky. His horse was in need of water and some rest. He'd passed a signpost a few miles back that told him he was twenty miles from the town of Gallows, but the horse was worn out. All he needed was a couple of hours and then he could make the rest of the trip.

There was a well right outside the house, but he knew how people were about their water, especially on a small spread. He needed to get permission from the owner before he tried to use it. He'd seen men die over less than a bucket of water. He also noticed that there were three horses tied off in front of the house. He didn't know what he was riding into. All the more reason to ride into it carefully.

He wanted his horse to walk slowly toward the water, but the animal could smell it and was headstrong to get to it. Lancaster took strong hold of the reins, though, and kept the animal from rushing in. They could wait the few minutes it would take to find the owner.

As he approached the house, though, the feeling of luck quickly turned to something else as the door to the house opened and three men dragged a dark-haired woman outside with them.

"Bitch!" one of them shouted. "I never did trust her."

"We'll make her pay now," another man said.

They dragged her toward the well. Lancaster wondered whether they were intending to throw her in. He found it odd that while the men were shouting at her, cursing and taunting her, the woman was not resisting, and was not making a sound. Then again, she probably felt that, as outnumbered as she was, it was futile to fight them.

All three men were wearing trail clothes, minus hats, and were carrying sidearms. If he intervened on behalf of the woman he was going to have to be ready to deal with three armed men. On the other hand, he didn't have much of a choice. He couldn't just watch them chuck her down the well, or worse, kill her.

He gigged his horse and trotted the last fifty feet, which brought him right up to them. At the sound of the horse the three men stopped and looked at him. They all released the woman, who slumped to the ground. Lancaster could see that her eyes were open, but he took his eyes away from her and put them on the three men. Looking at the woman too long could end up getting him killed.

"Looks like some excitement," Lancaster said. "Mind if I water my horse before you finish up?"

GALLOWS

Chapter One

Lancaster spotted the house and felt lucky. His horse was in need of water and some rest. He'd passed a signpost a few miles back that told him he was twenty miles from the town of Gallows, but the horse was worn out. All he needed was a couple of hours and then he could make the rest of the trip.

There was a well right outside the house, but he knew how people were about their water, especially on a small spread. He needed to get permission from the owner before he tried to use it. He'd seen men die over less than a bucket of water. He also noticed that there were three horses tied off in front of the house. He didn't know what he was riding into. All the more reason to ride into it carefully.

He wanted his horse to walk slowly toward the water, but the animal could smell it and was headstrong to get to it. Lancaster took strong hold of the reins, though, and kept the animal from rushing in. They could wait the few minutes it would take to find the owner.

As he approached the house, though, the feeling of luck quickly turned to something else as the door to the house opened and three men dragged a dark-haired woman outside with them.

"Bitch!" one of them shouted. "I never did trust her."

"We'll make her pay now," another man said.

They dragged her toward the well. Lancaster wondered whether they were intending to throw her in. He found it odd that while the men were shouting at her, cursing and taunting her, the woman was not resisting, and was not making a sound. Then again, she probably felt that, as outnumbered as she was, it was futile to fight them.

All three men were wearing trail clothes, minus hats, and were carrying sidearms. If he intervened on behalf of the woman he was going to have to be ready to deal with three armed men. On the other hand, he didn't have much of a choice. He couldn't just watch them chuck her down the well, or worse, kill her.

He gigged his horse and trotted the last fifty feet, which brought him right up to them. At the sound of the horse the three men stopped and looked at him. They all released the woman, who slumped to the ground. Lancaster could see that her eyes were open, but he took his eyes away from her and put them on the three men. Looking at the woman too long could end up getting him killed.

"Looks like some excitement," Lancaster said. "Mind if I water my horse before you finish up?"

the horse with a perfect killing shot. It was all Lancaster could do to roll away and keep from being pinned.

The youngest man had been startled by the gunplay and went for his gun way too late.

"Don't do it!" Lancaster yelled at him, getting to one knee.

The young man paid him no mind, probably didn't even hear the warning because of the blood pounding in his ears. Lancaster had to choice but to shoot him, which he did. He managed to dispatch all three men with three shots, which was the kind of shooting that had made his reputation many years ago, when he was plying his trade as a killer for hire.

"Damn it, I told you not to!" he shouted as the boy fell onto his face.

Lancaster got to his feet and quickly approached the fallen men, kicking their pistols away just in case, but he needn't have bothered.

They were all dead.

Chapter Two

Lancaster was a creature of habit. Before he did anything else he ejected the spent shells from his gun, replaced them with live loads and then holstered the gun. Only then did he bend over and drag the woman out from under the dead man.

As he carried her to the porch he noticed that her dress, face and hands were covered with blood. He set her down in a rocking chair on the porch and inspected her for injuries, but found none. The blood obviously belonged to somebody else, but who?

"Ma'am, can you hear me?"

Her eyes were open, but she didn't respond. He considered his options. Get her some water from the well, or go inside the house and see what awaited him there?

"Ma'am?" He tried again, but to no avail.

He made up his mind, stood up and entered the house. He was immediately greeted by the smell of blood, a scent he was very familiar with.

He was standing just inside the door, with a kitchen set up on the left with a table and chairs, and to his right a sofa, armchair and fireplace. Wherever the blood smell was coming from, it wasn't from here. There was another doorway, and from where he stood he could see the foot of a bed.

He crossed the room and entered the bedroom. At first all he saw was the blood spatter on the wall, but then he spotted the boots sticking out from the other side of the bed. It took only three steps, and then he was looking down at the bloody body of a man who had obviously taken a shotgun blast to the head. This was the only place he could see that the woman would have gotten the blood all over her. Was this her husband? Perhaps the three men killed him, and then she had cradled his body in her arms, covering herself with his blood.

He went back into the main room, grabbed a couple of tin cups from the kitchen. He then went back outside, where the woman was still in the chair, rocking back and forth slowly.

He walked to the well, brought the bucket up, filled the two cups and carried them to the porch.

"Here," he said, holding one cup to the woman's mouth. He tried to get her to drink, but without much success. He sipped a bit from the other cup himself, then set both cups down on the porch and went back inside. He searched the kitchen and living room area, finally found a bottle of whiskey in a cupboard.

He carried the bottle outside, picked up one cup and splashed the contents into the woman's face. Thankfully she reacted, blinked, sputtered a bit as the water caused some of the blood on her face to rinse off.

Lancaster poured some whiskey into the empty cup, then held it to the woman's mouth. She sipped and choked, but he held the cup there, lifting it until she had swallowed it all. He then lifted the bottle to his own mouth and took a healthy swig.

He crouched down next to her and could see that her eyes were focusing.

"Ma'am, can you hear me?"

"Y-yes."

"I just rode up here lookin' for some water," he said, "and now I've killed three men. Can you tell me what happened here?"

"My husband—"

"The man inside?"

"Yes."

"I'm sorry, but he's dead."

"I know."

"Did those men kill him?" he asked. "And then drag you outside?"

"No."

"No? They didn't kill your husband?"

"N-no, they didn't," she said.

"Well, if they didn't kill him, who did?" Lancaster asked.

"I did," she said. "M-may I have some more whiskey, please?"

Chapter Three

Lancaster knew the law was going to have to come out to this ranch, so he didn't move any of the bodies. But he did have to get his saddle off his dead horse, then pick one of the three dead men's horses to ride into town. He took the best of the three, a steel dust that looked about five or six years old. He took off the old saddle, replaced it with his own. After that he had to choose one of the other horses for the woman to ride.

After another nip of whiskey the woman told him her name was Liz Burkett. Her husband's name was Harry Burkett. He couldn't get much more out of her, though, so he still didn't know who the three dead men were. He also still didn't know why she killed her husband, or if she had, in fact, actually killed him and wasn't just in shock.

It would have been nice to get her out of her bloody clothes, but she would have had to go back inside to change, and she wasn't about to do that.

"I ain't goin' back inside," she said again and again, until he finally told her she didn't have to.

He got a bucket of water from the well and carried it over to the porch. With a cloth he got from the kitchen he tried his best to clean the blood from her face, neck, arms and hands. There was some in her hair, but he couldn't do anything about that. While cleaning her face and arms he thought it was odd when he found some fading bruises, as well as scars.

When he had her relatively clean and the two horses saddled, he said, "We're gonna have to go into town now, Mrs. Burkett. We have to go and talk to the sheriff, and get you to a doctor."

She just nodded without comment.

He got her to her feet and over to the horse. He gathered her dress up so she could mount the horse the traditional way and not have to ride sidesaddle. He averted his eyes even though she was beyond modesty.

He walked around and mounted the other horse, then turned and looked back at the scene behind him. Four dead men, three by his hand, and he still had no clue what had happened in that house.

He grabbed up her horse's reins, because she was in no condition to handle the reins herself, and led her horse away from her home.

He got an eerie feeling as they road into the town of Gallows, New Mexico.

He knew that strangers riding into town often attracted suspicious stares, but it wasn't him the people of Gallows were staring at; it was the woman. It was if they knew she had killed her husband and reviled her for it—only how could they know?

He led her down the street, and she didn't seem to be noticing anything along the way. He spotted the sheriff's office, but wondered whether he should first take her to see a doctor.

Gallows was a midsized town, and he doubted they'd have more than one doctor. He decided to stop someone to ask.

"Excuse me," he called out t a man, who ignored him and kept walking.

He tried again.

"Excuse me, ma'am," he called, but the woman ducked her head and scurried away.

He gigged his horse, caught up to a man who was hurrying across the street and grabbed him by the back of the collar.

"Hey!" the man shouted.

"I'm only gonna ask this once!" Lancaster said to the man. "Where's the doctor's office?"

"Down the street two blocks, then right," the man said, "Leggo!"

"Much obliged."

The man hurried off, as if he was afraid someone might have seen him talk to Lancaster.

Grabbing up the reins of the woman's horse again, he headed past the sheriff's office and, following the man's reluctant directions, reined in both horses in front of the doctor's office.

The shingle said DOCTOR OTTO MEADE. He hoped that the doctor would not be like the people on the street, and slam the door in his face.

"Is that Mrs. Burkett?" the white-haired man who answered the door said.

"Yes, sir. She needs treatment."

"She usually does," the doctor said. "Bring her right in here, sir."

The doctor led the way through a waiting room to an examining room.

"Leave her here," he said. "I'll examine her. You can wait outside."

"I have to go over to the sheriff's office, Doc," Lancaster said. "I'll check back on her after that."

"Wait, wait," the doctor said. "Before you go, what's your name?"

"Lancaster."

"Are you a friend of Mrs. Burkett?"

"I don't even know her," Lancaster said. "I rode up to her ranch to ask for water and got involved."

"In what?"

"That's what I have to talk to the sheriff about, Doc," Lancaster said, "and I've got to do that first. After that I'll answer whatever questions you have."

"You're a stranger in this town," the older man said. "I'd advise you to tread lightly."

"I think the ship has sailed on that advice, Doc," Lancaster said. "I assume you know this lady?"

"Yes, I've treated Mrs. Burkett before. I assume her husband was involved?"

"Yeah," Lancaster said, "her husband was real involved, but it's a pretty safe bet that he ain't gonna be involved anymore."

Chapter Four

Lancaster left both horses in front of the doctor's office and walked to the sheriff's. Along the way he attracted some attention because he was a stranger and because he was a tall man who walked with confidence, but not nearly as much attention as he had attracted when he was riding with Liz Burkett.

When he reached the sheriff's office there was a wooden shingle outside, and it looked as if it had been crafted by the same person who made the doctor's. It said SHERIFF MATTHEW JESSUP. He entered without knocking.

The interior was nothing unusual—a desk, a pot-bellied stove, a file cabinet, a gun rack and a doorway that most likely led to a cellblock. The thing that was unusual was that the place was clean—spotless, in fact. He'd never been in a sheriff's or marshal's office that clean before.

The man behind the desk went along with the cleanliness of the place. He was wearing a clean blue shirt and a black tie. On a hat rack behind him was a Stetson that matched the tie. He had black hair going a little gray at the temples, and a black mustache. He looked like a man in his forties who had kept himself in good shape. Lancaster hoped that the man's age meant he would be dealing with an experienced lawman.

The second man in the room was a deputy, young and not as well kept as the sheriff or the office. He looked to be in his late twenties, and eyed Lancaster with suspicion.

"Afternoon," the lawman said in a deep baritone. "Can I help ya?"

"I hope so, Sheriff," Lancaster said. "My name's Lancaster. I just drove into town with a woman named Liz Burkett."

"I know Liz," the man said. "Somethin' wrong?"

"Somethin's real wrong," Lancaster said. "I rode up to the Burkett place to ask if I cold water my horse just as three men were draggin' her out of her house. She was all bloody, and they had some bad intentions."

"What happened?"

"I tried to talk them out of whatever they were gonna do, but they were bound and determined to hurt the lady," Lancaster explained—and hoped he was explaining it well enough to justify his actions.

"And?"

"And they threw down on me," he said. "I had no choice."

"You killed 'em?" the sheriff asked.

"Yes, sir."

"All three?"

15

"Yes, sir."

"Take a hit yourself, did ya?"

"No, but they killed my horse. I took two of their horses so I could ride in and bring the lady with me."

"Liz's in town?"

"Yes, sir, she's at the doctor's office. We sure got some bad looks as we were ridin' in."

"Liz's not real popular in town, I'm afraid," the lawman said.

"Well, I hope that don't mean that three men could drag her out of her house and beat her—or worse, kill her."

"Nobody's got the right to do that," the lawman said, standing up. He was wearing a slick rig on his right hip, with a pearl-handled Colt in the holster. The leather and studs on the holster looked freshly oiled and cleaned. "Did you go in the house, Mr. Lancaster?"

"I did."

"And what did you find there?"

"Another dead man."

"You didn't kill this one?"

"No, sir."

"Do you know who did?"

"No, sir," he said without the slightest hesitation. He still wasn't sure Liz Burkett wasn't speaking out of shock, so he didn't want to repeat anything she had told him.

"And do you know who he was?"

"No, sir."

"Liz didn't say?"

"She didn't have much to say," Lancaster replied. "I asked her questions, but she wouldn't answer. I'm no doctor, but I believe the lady is in shock."

"You didn't take a look at the man? Maybe go through his pockets?"

"Sheriff, there were four dead men out there," Lancaster explained, "and all I did was check them to see if they were dead."

The Sheriff seemed to consider all the information before speaking again.

"Mr. Lancaster, I'm gonna have to ask you for two things."

"What are they?" He was suddenly aware that the deputy had moved over behind him. "Whoa," he said, turning sideways so he could see both badge toters. "Ask your man not to do that, Sheriff."

"Do what?"

"I'd be obliged if you told him not to stand behind me. . . ."

"Hector," Jessup said, "move over to where the man can see ya."

"But Sheriff—"

"Just do it!"

The deputy moved a bit to his right and forward, so Lancaster could easily see him.

"Now, about those two things I need . . ." the sheriff said.

"Yeah?" Lancaster asked.

"I'll need you to ride out to the Burkett place with me and my deputy so we can see what we're dealin' with, here."

"That's no problem," Lancaster said. "And what's the second?"

"Well, I'll need you to hand over your gun," the sheriff said.

"Well, Sheriff," Lancaster said, "there I think we got us a little bit of a problem."

Chapter Five

"Now, just why would that be a problem, Mr. Lancaster?" the lawman asked.

"Well, for one thing, your deputy, there, is real itchy. For another, I'm a stranger in your town, and I wouldn't be real comfortable walking around naked."

"Don't worry," Sheriff Jessup said, "my deputy will keep his gun in its holster. And you don't have to worry about walkin' around naked, because you'll be under my protection."

"Why do you want my gun?" Lancaster asked.

"Well, you just told me you killed three men," Jessup said. "I've got to investigate the matter. Until I do, I can either put you in a cell or simply disarm you."

"I don't like either of those options."

"Now, look here, friend, the sheriff said—"

"The sheriff says shut up, Hector," Jessup said to his deputy.

The deputy quieted with a hurt look.

"Sheriff," Lancaster said, "why don't we just ride out there and you can see that everything is the way I said it was. Then when we come back you can question Mrs. Burkett. She'll tell you how everything happened."

"And after that?"

"Well, after that I don't think you'll want my gun," Lancaster said.

"And if I do?"

"We can talk about it then."

"Mr. Lancaster," Jessup asked, "what's the real reason you don't want to give up your gun?"

"Sheriff . . . does my name mean anything to you?" Lancaster asked after a moment's hesitation.

Jessup stared at him.

"It did, when you came in."

"Then you know why I can't walk around without my gun."

"What's he talkin' about, Sheriff?" the deputy asked. "Ya want me to take his gun from him?"

"Jesus Christ, Hector," Jessup said, "can't you just shut up?"

The sheriff turned around and grabbed his hat off the rack.

"All right, Lancaster," he said, "let's ride out to the Burkett place."

He headed for the door, followed by Lancaster and the deputy.

"Not you, Hector. You stay here at the office."

"But Sheriff—"

"Stay here!"

Jessup opened the door.

"Ya want me to go and talk to Liz, Sheriff?" Hector asked.

20

"I want you to do what I just told you to do, Hector," Jessup said. "Stay . . . here!"

Jessup and Lancaster stepped outside and closed the door.

"Where's your horse?" the sheriff asked.

"Over at the doctor's office."

"Okay," Jessup said. "I'll get my horse and meet you at the doctor's."

"Are you gonna talk to Mrs. Burkett before we go?" Lancaster asked.

"No," Jessup said, "after we get back."

"Okay, then I'll get my horse and meet you at the livery stable. Which one is it?"

"North end of town," the sheriff said. "Okay, I'll meet you at the livery."

"Say, Sheriff?"

"Yeah?"

"Why don't you want your deputy to come along with us?"

"Because you're right about him," Jessup said. "He's itchy."

Chapter Six

Lancaster and Jessup rode up to the Burkett house. Everything was just as Lancaster had left it. They dismounted and the sheriff walked over to the three dead men and the dead horse by the well.

"Do you see?" Lancaster asked. "One of them got a shot off at me and hit my horse."

"Yeah, I see."

Jessup turned and walked to the house. He went inside while Lancaster waited by the horses until the lawman came out.

"That's Harry Burkett, all right," he said. "I can tell, even though his head was blowed off."

"So he's her husband?"

"Yeah."

"So you see, it had to have happened the way I said," Lancaster commented.

"Maybe," Jessup said.

"What do you mean, maybe?"

"You got him, Hector?"

"I got him, Sheriff."

The voice came from behind him. Lancaster turned to look. The deputy was standing there with a rifle on him. When he turned back he was looking down the barrel of Sheriff Jessup's gun.

"What's goin' on, Sheriff?"

"I'll take your gun now, Lancaster."

"You went back and told your deputy to ride out here ahead of us," Lancaster said, "before I met you at the livery."

"That's right."

"Tricky."

"With a man like you," Jessup said, "I figured that was my only shot. Now, I could take the gun from your holster or have Hector take it, but I'm askin' you to give it to me."

"Until when?"

"Until I get this all sorted out."

"Why isn't it sorted out now?" Lancaster asked. "You can see what happened. All you have to do is talk to Mrs. Burkett."

"There's a little more to it than that."

"Like what?"

"I have two deputies," Jessup said. "One is Hector, there, and the other is—or was—Harry Burkett."

Lancaster stared at him, then said, "Okay, so the dead man was your deputy. I didn't kill him."

"That remains to be seen."

"He was shot in the house with a shotgun," Lancaster said, "before I even got here. I admit I shot the other three, but not him."

"Lancaster," Jessup said, "I don't wanna kill you, because I think you're probably right about all of it. But that's gonna be up to the judge."

"A judge?"

"No, not a judge," Jessup said. "*The* judge."

"Look—"

"I need the gun now," the sheriff said, "or we can't go any further."

Lancaster considered his options, decided he had only two choices. He could try to kill two lawmen, or give up his gun.

"All right, damn it!" he said.

He drew the gun, reversed it and held it out to the sheriff. He considered executing a border shift, but decided against it. The situation did not yet seem so hopeless that he would consider killing two lawmen.

"Thank you," Jessup said.

"You want to shackle me?"

"That won't be necessary. We can just mount up and ride back."

"What about the bodies."

"That'll be taken care of."

Suddenly there were four other men there. They went into the house, brought out the body of Harry Burkett covered in a blanket. They tied it to the horse that had been left there.

"We'll take Harry in with us," Jessup said. "The others will be brought in later."

Lancaster mounted up, followed by Sheriff Jessup. The deputy had to walk a ways to get to his horse. Lancaster and Jessup turned their horses and rode past the bodies, which were being moved.

"What about them?" Lancaster asked. "Were they deputies, too?"

"No," Jessup said.

Thank God they weren't lawmen, Lancaster thought.

"Then who were they?" he asked. "Do you know?"

"I know," Jessup said. "They were Deputy Burkett's brothers."

Chapter Seven

When Lancaster and Jessup rode into town with Harry Burkett's body tied to a saddle the town had already heard about Burkett's death. They glared at Lancaster, who was waiting for them to rush him. When one man did charge at him he had to give Jessup credit. The sheriff maneuvered his horse so that he put his foot against the man's chest and pushed him back.

"Don't try that again!" he shouted to the man he'd just knocked down, as well as to everyone else.

"Where are we going first?" Lancaster asked.

"My office. I'm gonna put you in a cell for your own good."

"I'd rather go to the doctor's office," he said. "I'd like to check on Mrs. Burkett, and maybe you can get her story."

"You'd be safer in a cell," Jessup said. "Harry was well liked in this town."

"I didn't kill him."

"His brothers were popular, too."

Lancaster fell silent.

"Well?"

"If I have a choice," Lancaster answered, "I choose the doctor."

"Okay," Jessup said. "I have to bring Harry's body to him anyway."

As they rode over to the doctor's office Lancaster said, "When I cleaned the blood from her face and arms I saw old bruises, scars. Did her husband beat her?"

"That's none of my business," Jessup said. "That's nobody's business but theirs."

"I'm just tryin' to think of a reason for her to blow his head off with a shotgun."

Jessup looked at him.

"You think she did it?"

"I'm just . . . wonderin'. . . ." He wished he had kept quiet.

"Did she say she killed him?" he asked.

"What? No, but if those other three were his brothers and they were draggin' her outside . . . I mean, they were gonna kill her, Sheriff, so they must've thought she did it."

"Jesus," Jessup said. "Do you know how respected the Burkett family is in this town? In all of Chavez County?"

"No, I don't."

"No," the lawman said, "of course you don't, but you're gonna find out."

When they entered the doctor's office, Dr. Meade looked up from his desk, removed the wire-framed glasses he was wearing.

"I was wonderin' when you'd get around to me," he said. He looked at Jessup. "Is it true?"

"It's true," Jessup said.

"All four?"

"Yes."

"All four?" Lancaster asked.

"Sons," Jessup said, "all four Burkett sons."

"Sons?"

"The judge's sons."

This just kept getting better and better.

"This judge, he's *the* judge you were talking about?" Lancaster asked.

"That's right."

"What about her?" Lancaster asked the doctor. "What about Mrs. Burkett?"

"You were right—she was in shock," he said. "I've sedated her."

"So we can't talk to her now?" Sheriff Jessup asked.

"You can't talk to her until tomorrow mornin'," the doctor said.

"Doctor, what about those old bruises and scars?" Lancaster asked.

The doctor looked at Lancaster, then at Jessup.

"That's not for us to talk about," Jessup said.

"Did she say anything before you sedated her?" Lancaster asked.

Again, the doctor looked at the lawman.

"All she said was that you saved her life."

"There!" Lancaster said to Jessup. "That should be enough for you."

"You'll still be safer in a cell," Jessup said.

The door to the doctor's office opened and the deputy, Hector, walked in.

"They're comin' in with the other bodies, Sheriff," he said.

"Okay," Jessup said, "take Mr. Lancaster and put him in a cell."

"Sheriff—" Lancaster started.

"Keep your distance from him," Jessup told the deputy, "and if he tries to escape, shoot him in the leg. You got that?"

"I got it, Sheriff," the deputy said, drawing his gun.

Jessup looked at Lancaster.

"Don't forget what we said about Hector," he said. "He's itchy."

Chapter Eight

Lancaster walked to the sheriff's office and allowed the deputy to put him in a cell. As the deputy turned the key in the lock he got all puffed up, so Lancaster decided to teach him a lesson. He reached out and quickly grabbed the deputy's gun from his holster before the younger man could move out of reach.

"Hey, wha—" the deputy said, his eyes going wide as Lancaster showed him the barrel of his own gun.

"You're a little too full of yourself, boy," Lancaster said.

The deputy swallowed hard.

"What's your name?"

"H-Hector."

"Your full name."

"Hector A-Adams."

"Well, Deputy Adams, you're not gonna last too long in this job if you're this careless. I could force you to give me the keys now, and then either leave you locked in here for your boss to find, or just kill you."

Now the young man tried to swallow, but his mouth was too dry.

"But I'm not gonna do either," Lancaster said. He reversed the gun in his hand and held it out to the deputy, butt first.

The deputy stared at it, suspicious of a trick.

"Go ahead, take it."

Slowly the deputy reached out and then, at the last minute, he snatched the gun away, then backed up a few feet before holstering it.

"W-what'd you do that for?" he asked. "You coulda got away."

"Why would I want to get away?" Lancaster asked. "I didn't do anything wrong."

"That don't matter," Deputy Adams said. "You killed Judge Burkett's boys. It's gonna be hard for you to get a fair trial, if you even make it to court."

"The judge's court," Lancaster said. "The father of the men I killed."

"That's right," the deputy said, "but you may not make it."

"Well, that would be your job, son," Lancaster said. "You might have to hold off the whole town to get me to court."

"Yeah, well . . . what you told the sheriff?"

"What was that?"

"You asked him if he knew your name," the deputy said. "You somebody famous?"

"Ask your boss that, kid," Lancaster said. "I'm much too modest to say."

"Well . . ." The deputy looked really confused. "Uh, thanks for, uh, givin' me my gun back."

31

"Just a lesson, Deputy," Lancaster said. "Learn from it."

"Yes, sir."

The deputy backed out of the cellblock.

"Yeah, that's Harry Burkett," the doctor told the sheriff. "I've patched him up enough times to recognize the body."

"Shit!"

"You got to and tell the judge."

"He probably knows already."

"And Lancaster killed the other three boys?" the doctor asked.

"That's what he says."

"That's what Liz said, too," the doctor said.

"What else did she say?"

"Just that Harry's brothers were gonna kill her, and that man Lancaster saved her life. Lancaster . . . Don't I know that name?"

"He was a gun for hire years ago," the sheriff said, "then dropped out of sight."

'Maybe he's back in business."

"And who woulda hired him to kill the Burketts?" Sheriff Jessup asked.

"Maybe Liz?"

"Why?"

"Come on, Sheriff," the doctor said, "you know Harry used to beat on her—"

"That's their business, Doc," Jessup said. "I don't get involved in the problems a married couple is havin'."

"That poor girl took a lot of beating from Harry—" the doctor started, but Jessup cut him off quickly.

"Doc! What part of *I don't get involved* don't you understand?" he demanded.

"Okay, okay," the doctor said. "I'm just sayin'—"

"Well, don't say it where I can hear it," Sheriff Jessup said. "Was that on the level, what you said about not talkin' to her until tomorrow mornin'?"

"Yes," the sawbones said. "Why would I lie about that?"

"I don't know," Jessup said. "Yeah, okay, I've got to go and talk to the judge."

"I'll arrange for the body to be taken to the undertaker."

"You do that, Doc," Jessup said. "Put him with his brothers."

Doctor Meade said, "I don't envy you the job of tellin' the judge about Lancaster. What do you think he's gonna do?"

"I don't know, Doc," Jessup said. "I stopped tryin' to predict what the judge was gonna do a long time ago."

Chapter Nine

This wasn't the first time Lancaster had ever been in a cell. He felt certain that Liz Burkett was going to clear him of any wrongdoing as soon as she was able to talk to the sheriff, so he wasn't feeling any of the nerves the occupants of a cell usually felt. He sat down on the bunk and relaxed for the first time in days. He decided to lie down and get some rest while he was there. At least he wouldn't have to pay for a hotel.

Maybe he'd even spend the night, and then they'd have to feed him. Being in jail wasn't such a bad thing, after all.

Matt Jessup stepped into the judge's office, prepared for the worst. Judge William Burkett was in his sixties, but was still a strapping man who stood over six feet, with a barrel chest and large hands. Often he'd use his hands to bring order to his court when he'd misplaced his gavel.

He was sitting behind his desk now, watching as Jessup crossed the room, hat in hand.

"Matthew."

"Judge."

"Want to tell me what happened?"

"Fact is, Judge," Jessup said, "I don't rightly know yet."

"My boys are dead," the judge said. "You know that much."

"Yeah, I know that much."

"And you know who killed them."

"I know who killed Luke, Tom and Ben," Jessup said. "I don't know yet who killed Harry."

"Tell me about it," the judge said. "Sit."

Jessup sat and told the judge Lancaster's story, just the way it had been told to him.

"What does Liz have to say?" the judge asked.

"Nothin'," Jessup said. "The doc says I can't talk to her until tomorrow mornin'."

"Is she in shock?"

"Yes."

"Where is she?"

"At the doc's."

"Have her taken to my house," the judge said. "Mrs. Burkett will look after her."

"Do you think that's wise, Judge?"

"Why not?"

"Well . . . there's a chance . . . just a small chance . . . that Liz might've killed Harry."

"What reason would she have had to do that?" the judge asked.

"I don't know," Jessup said, "but just in case she has to come up in front of you . . . on trial, I mean . . ."

"I see what you mean," the judge said. "All right,

35

get her a room in a hotel—the Dutchman. The best room they have, and I'll pay for it."

The Dutchman Hotel was the newest and best hotel in Gallows. The best room they had would not be cheap.

"All right," Jessup said. "I'll talk to the doc."

He stood up.

"Where is Lancaster now?"

"In a cell."

"What's his background?"

"He used to be a gun for hire, years ago," Jessup said. "Now he's just . . . a drifter."

"Still good with a gun, though," the judge said, "if he gunned my three boys."

"Your boys weren't gunman, Judge," Jessup said. "With what Lancaster is or used to be, they didn't have a chance."

"Even at three-to-one odds?" the judge asked.

"Even then, Judge."

"Well," the judge said, "I'll want to talk to this Lancaster in the morning. Bring him here first thing."

"Yes, sir."

"And we'll talk to Liz," he said. "We'll find out what really happened out there today. We'll find out why my boys are dead."

"Yes, sir."

Jessup started for the door, then turned.

"Um, Mrs. Burkett—she doesn't know yet, does she?" he asked.

"No," the judge said. "I'll be telling her tonight,

so your suggestion that Liz not go to my house is really a very good one, Matthew. Thank you."

"Sure, Judge," Jessup said. "Sure."

"I have work to do now, Sheriff," the judge said. "I'll see you in the morning."

"Yes, sir," Jessup said. "First thing."

"After breakfast will do," the judge said. "Give your prisoner a hearty breakfast, and then bring him here."

"Yes, sir, Judge," Sheriff Jessup said, and left.

Chapter Ten

Lancaster was awake when the sheriff came into the office.

"Sheriff?"

Jessup stuck his head though the door.

"How's Mrs. Burkett?" Lancaster asked. "It's been hours."

"She's restin'," Jessup said. "We moved her to one of the hotels."

"Oh, that's good," Lancaster said. "I know she didn't want to go back into that house."

"Nobody's gonna make her go back if she don't want to," Jessup said.

"What about me?" Lancaster asked. "Am I going to be in here all night?"

"Looks like," Jessup said. "The judge wants to see you in the mornin'."

"Good," Lancaster said. "Am I to be fed?"

"I'll bring you some supper," Jessup said. "Breakfast, too, from the café down the street."

"Any good?"

"Good enough," Jessup said. "I eat there. I got work to do, though. I'll see you in about an hour."

"Fine with me," Lancaster said. "I'll be here."

Jessup withdrew. Lancaster sat back down, then stood up and walked to the barred window. His only view was of a back alley. Nothing to see, but easy access for somebody who might want to take a shot at him.

He moved the packet from where it was into a back corner of the cell. Somebody with a gun would have to reach in to try to get a shot off. He'd be able to grab for the gun.

Not that he was expecting an attack, but he wouldn't have been surprised by one, once the word passed that he'd killed three of the Burkett boys, who were supposed to be well liked. He wondered whether those were different words for "feared." Those boys had an arrogance about them, an arrogance he had seen in men many times before—even in himself, when he was younger. Only he'd lasted long enough to outlive it.

They hadn't.

Not his fault, but he'd walked into something he wasn't going to be able to just walk away from.

All to water a horse that ended up dead.

Jessup came walking into the cellblock an hour later, carrying a tray covered with a red and white checked napkin.

"Supper," he said.

"Finally," Lancaster said, sitting up. "I'm starving."

He remained seated, with his back against the rear wall.

"You've been in a cell before," Jessup said, opening the barred door.

"In my younger days," Lancaster said. "Learned to stay back so the sheriff could open the door and feed me."

Jessup walked up to him and put the tray down next to him.

"I'm not worried about you tryin' to escape," he said. "At least not yet."

"Not until I talk to the judge, huh?"

"That's beef stew," Jessup said, backing out of the cell and locking the door. "Gave you a spoon to eat it with."

"No fork?" Lancaster took the napkin off the tray. Bowl of beef stew, big hunk of corn bread, piece of apple pie.

"Guess I don't trust you quite that much," Jessup said.

"I can handle all of this with a spoon," Lancaster said. "Thanks."

"Sure."

Jessup left. Lancaster picked up the bowl and spoon. The bowl still had a lot of warmth. He tasted the stew, found it to be a bit tasteless, but edible.

Jessup came back in at that point, held a canteen through the bars.

"Forgot to give you somethin' to drink."

Lancaster got up, accepted the canteen.

"Thanks."

"How's the stew?"

"It's fine."

40

"They bake better than they cook," Jessup said. "The corn bread will be better, and the pie even better than that. Enjoy."

"Thanks, Sheriff," Lancaster said. "Thanks for being decent. It can't be easy, losing a friend."

"A friend?" Jessup said. "Harry Burkett was not my friend."

"A colleague, then."

"Yeah," Jessup said, "a colleague."

Well, well, Lancaster thought, sitting back down.

Chapter Eleven

"Are you telling me that someone killed our sons?" Mildred Burkett asked her husband. "All four of our sons? *My* sons?"

Judge Burkett poured himself an evening cognac and turned to face his wife. She was sixty-five, and her face had fallen many years ago. Her body, once tall and proud, was misshapen and shrunken beneath her dress. Burkett knew he should've gone to see his mistress tonight instead of coming home. He would have, too, if someone hadn't killed his four sons.

"Are you even human?" she asked him. "Aren't you the least bit upset?"

"Of course I'm upset, Mildred."

"Where is the man who killed them?"

"He's in jail."

"You're going to hang him, aren't you?"

"Not without a trial."

"A trial?" she asked. "The nearest tree is all the trial he deserves."

"Mildred—"

"Where did it happen?"

"Out at Harry's place."

"Liz . . ." Mildred said. "Where is she?"

"She's at the hotel," Burkett told her. "The doctor has sedated her. She was in shock."

"Shock," Mildred said, "right. She had something to do with this. The man is probably a . . . a lover. They were probably having a tawdry affair and Harry found out."

"Then why would his brothers be out there?" the judge asked.

"For moral support—what else?"

The judge knew there was very little that was moral about his sons. Luke, Tom and Ben were layabouts. Harry was a deputy only because the judge had forced Jessup to pin a badge on him.

"I'll have to find out what happened before I make any ruling, Mildred."

"A ruling? About our sons?"

"Mildred, you're becoming overwrought. I can have the doctor come out and sedate you."

"You'd like that, wouldn't you?" she asked. "You'd like me to be sedated."

The judge's head was suddenly pounding.

"What I'd like, Mildred," he said, touching his fingertips to his forehead, "is for you to shut up."

"Having one of your headaches, William?" Mildred said. "You know the cure for your headaches, don't you?" She moved closer to him. "It's hitting me, remember? When you hit me you feel better."

"Mildred, don't push me."

"Why? Because you'll break my jaw again, like last year? When we told the doctor I fell down the stairs?"

"Mildred, damn it!" The judge raised his hand as if to deliver a backhanded blow.

"Go ahead, Will! My boys are dead. Kill me, and then you'll have it the way you always wanted it. You'll be alone. You and that . . . whore!"

He delivered a measured blow. The only damage it did was a split lip.

"Go and get my dinner on the table," he said, holding her chin in his hand, "but clean yourself up first."

She jerked her chin from his hand and backed away. It was the first time she had ever done that.

"You get your own dinner," she said. "My boys are dead. I have no reason to serve you anymore."

She turned and walked out of the room.

The judge looked down at the liquid in his glass. He drained it, went to the sideboard and poured another, then drank it while looking around his den, his private sanctum.

If she wasn't going to make him dinner, what reason did he have to stay? He finished his cognac, went to find Ronald, his manservant, to tell him to hitch up his buggy.

After the judge rode off, Ronald went back into the house. He was a black man in his sixties who had been working for Judge Burkett for forty years.

When he closed the front door he heard something from the bowels of the house. A woman, crying. He'd heard that sound before, but this time it was different. This time the woman sounded not as if she was in pain, but as if she was in agony.

He followed the sound, found Mrs. Burkett in her bedroom—the private bedroom that she did not share with her husband.

"Ma'am," he asked, "is you okay?"

Mildred Burkett looked up at Ronald, tears streaking her face.

"My boys are dead, Ronald," she said. "All my boys are dead."

"Don't worry, missus," he said. "The judge will see to it."

Her eyes flashed and she shouted, "Get out, you useless nigger! Get out!"

She pushed the confused man into the hall and slammed the door in his face. Then the crying resumed.

Chapter Twelve

"I'm tellin' ya," said Deputy Hector Adams, "we got the guy in a cell. His name is Lancaster. He's a gun for hire."

"You mean somebody hired him to kill the judge's boys?" Eddie Pratt asked.

Pratt was the deputy's best friend. He and the deputy were in a small saloon where they usually drank together, because the sheriff didn't want Adams drinking where people could see him.

"You got an image to uphold, Hector," Jessup would tell him. "You can't be drunk in public— you can't be drinkin' with your buddies. You might have to lock them up some night."

So he and Pratt, they drank in this little place on a side street, which usually had so few customers they didn't even know how it stayed open.

Pratt poured two more glasses of whiskey and put the bottle down on the table.

"If he's in a cell, what are ya waitin' for?" Pratt asked. "Let's get a rope and string him up."

"I can't do that, Eddie," Adams said. "I'm a goddamn deputy."

"And so was Harry Burkett," Pratt said. "You know, Harry had a lot of friends in town, Hector."

"I know that," the deputy said.

"Well," Pratt said, "I'll have to have a talk with them. Maybe this fella Lancaster won't make it out of his cell."

"Ya gotta stop talkin' like that, Eddie," Deputy Adams said. "I'll have to run ya in."

"Yeah, you and what army."

Both men started laughing, and then Pratt poured two more glasses of whiskey.

Jessup came in to pick up the empty tray.

"How was the pie?"

"Like you said," Lancaster said. "The corn bread was good, the pie better."

"They do a decent bacon and eggs," Jessup said. "I'll bring it in the morning, around eight. After that, we'll go and see the judge."

"How did the judge take it, Sheriff?"

"The judge? Like he takes most things."

"How's that?"

"Calm."

"The judge is a calm man?"

"Yes."

"All the time?"

"Yeah, why?"

"Just wondering if he'd fly off the handle."

"Not the judge. Not in his office, not in court. He'd die first."

"I guess that's good to know," Lancaster said. "Won't sentence me to hang on a whim."

47

"Oh, he might," Jessup said, "but he'd do it calmly."

Lancaster was starting to wonder whether letting himself be put into a cell was such a good idea.

Jessup put the tray in a corner. He'd take it back in the morning when he went to pick up breakfast. He checked his watch. Where the hell was Hector? If he was drunk again he was going to have to take his badge away from him. This would be a bad time for it, with Harry Burkett dead, but to tell the truth, no deputies would have been better than having both Hector and Harry. He hired Hector because nobody else wanted the job, and he hired Harry Burkett because the judge made him.

Lancaster was lying on his back when he saw the gun poke through the bars. He hadn't expected it to happen so soon, but he was ready. He reached up and grabbed the gun just as the owner pulled the trigger. One shot, and he pulled it from the man's hand. He jumped up on the bunk and peered out the window, but in the dark all he saw was a man running away. But he also smelled whiskey— a lot of it.

"Sheriff?" He walked to the front of the cell. "Sheriff!"

Jessup came running into the cellblock.

"I was out front," he said. "What happened?"

"Don't overreact," Lancaster said, and showed him the gun in his hand. He held it with the butt forward.

"What the hell?"

Lancaster handed the gun to Jessup.

"Somebody stuck his hand in the window with the gun, between the bars."

"How did you see it?" Jessup asked. "Wait, you moved that bed."

"Right," Lancaster said.

"You expected this?"

"Let's just say I'm not surprised," Lancaster said. "Your deputy told me how well liked those Burkett boys were."

"Did you see who it was?"

"Just a man running away into the darkness," Lancaster said. "Do the Burketts have other family?"

"Other family, yeah, and some friends," Jessup said. "But despite what my deputy told you, the Burkett boys didn't have that many friends."

"But the judge?"

"Now, that's different," the lawman said. "The judge is a hero in this town. He has a lot of friends, even more admirers."

"So this could've been any of them," Lancaster said. "Friend, admirer, family member?"

"I don't think any of the Burkett cousins would be that dumb," Jessup said.

"Well, I got a big whiff of whiskey, so that may have had some influence on how dumb, or brave, this man was."

"Brave?" Jessup asked. "How brave is it to shoot a man lying in a cell?" He hefted the gun in his hand. "You could have used this to get away."

"Believe me, I thought about it," Lancaster said, "for a split second, but then I'd be on the run. I think I'll hold my decisions until I talk to the judge."

"Well . . . thanks for not blowin' a hole in me. You want to move to another cell?"

"No," Lancaster said. "I don't think they'll be back. Not tonight, anyway. And after I talk to the judge tomorrow morning, I may be out of here."

"I wouldn't count on bein' any safer on the street," the sheriff said.

"At least I'd have my gun," Lancaster said. "I'd take my chances."

Chapter Thirteen

The rest of the night passed without incident. Deputy Adams never appeared, so Jessup and Lancaster both slept in the jail—one in the office, the other in a cell. In the morning Jessup made a pot of coffee, brought Lancaster a cup, then walked down to the café to pick up breakfast for both of them. Jessup ate with Lancaster, sitting just outside the cell. They talked a bit about their pasts and their presents. Lancaster found himself telling Jessup about how accidentally killing a little girl during a gunfight changed his life.

"I don't know that I could've crawled out of a bottle after that," Jessup said.

"What about this job?" Lancaster asked.

"I've worn a badge all over the West, but towns outgrow you, and you move on. I think this is my last stop. Especially after workin' with—or for—the judge."

"For?"

"He pretty much runs the town," Jessup said. "The county."

"Does he have ambitions of going further? Like to the state capital?"

"You'd think so, wouldn't ya? But he doesn't seem to. I think he's happy here."

"Is his wife alive?"

"Yeah, but they—they're hardly ever seen together. He's got a mistress he doesn't think anyone knows about. Jesus, why am I tellin' you all this?"

"Just between you and me, Sheriff," Lancaster said, "I think you might be looking for a way out. What was the relationship of the judge with his boys like?"

"He used them like his own little army," Jessup said. "To get his way."

"And the people in town like him?"

"Like him, fear him," Jessup said, "to a lot of people here it's all the same."

"How did Harry Burkett become a deputy?"

"The judge wanted him to be," Jessup said. "I didn't have a choice at the time."

"Maybe," Lancaster said, "you have a choice now."

"Maybe," Jessup said, standing up. "I've said too much. I still have a job to do."

"Like taking me over to see the judge?"

"Yeah, and like firing that drunken deputy of mine. It wouldn't surprise me if he's the cause of somebody tryin' to shoot you last night."

'Why do you say that?"

"Because he gets drunk and starts yappin', that's why. I've told him you can't be a lawman and stay out gettin' drunk with your friends, too.

He probably told one of them about you, and that's why they made a try for you."

"So you're going to be down two deputies," Lancaster said.

"Looks like it. Okay, come on," Jessup said, opening the cell door. "It's time to go and see the judge."

"Will you stay in the office when we talk, him and me?" Lancaster asked.

"Probably not," Sheriff Jessup said. "The judge likes to conduct his business alone—that is, if it ain't in a courtroom."

"No witnesses, huh?"

Jessup shrugged. "That might be it."

Jessup gave Lancaster back his hat and vest, but not his gun.

"Walk ahead of me, Lancaster," Jessup said. "I'll watch your back."

"I hope you do a good job of it, Sheriff."

Chapter Fourteen

Judge Burkett was waiting for them.

As they entered his office he turned away from the window to face them. He had watched them walk down the block to his building, watched the man who had gunned down three of his sons and may have killed the fourth.

"Is this him?" he asked.

"Judge Burkett," Jessup said. "This is Lancaster."

"No first name?"

"Lancaster's a pretty long name," Lancaster said. "Never figured there'd be room for a first on a headstone."

Burkett nodded. "Okay, Sheriff," he said, "you can wait just outside. If Mr. Lancaster decides to attack me, I'll call." He opened the top drawer of his desk and took out a gun. "Or I'll just shoot him myself."

"Nobody's going to have to shoot me," Lancaster said. "Mind if I sit?"

"Please do. Sheriff?"

"I'll be right outside." Lancaster didn't know

whether the sheriff was talking to him or the judge.

Lancaster waited while the judge got himself comfortable behind his desk. The man took a cigar from a box, clipped off the end, then got it going to his satisfaction, the air around his head filling with smoke. He did not offer Lancaster one.

"Now then," he said, "why don't you tell me how you came to kill all my boys?"

Liz Burkett woke with a start, sat up in bed and stared about her wildly. Dr. Otto Meade happened to be in the room at the time, getting ready to examine her.

"It's all right, Mrs. Burkett," he said, moving toward the bed. "It's all right. You're safe."

"Where am I?"

"You're in town," Doc Meade said, "in the hotel. The Dutchman."

"In town?"

"Yes," he said. "Do you remember anythin' that happened yesterday?"

"Yesterday . . ." she said, putting her hand to her head. "Yesterday . . ."

"Out at your place?" the doc asked. "A . . . shooting?"

"A shooting," she said, then clutched her head in her hands. "Oh, my God!"

"Now, now," Meade said, "just lie back. I want to examine you."

She lay on her back, and he raised the nightgown

she was wearing—one the hotel had been able to provide for her—so he could probe her abdomen. He'd noticed fresh bruising there the day before, an indication that someone had punched her in the stomach.

"He's dead, isn't he?" she asked.

"Who?"

"Harry, my husband."

"Yes, Mr. Burkett's dead."

"And the others? His brothers?"

"Also dead."

She tried to sit up abruptly, but the movement caused pain in her abdomen and she fell back down with a sharp intake of breath.

"Now, take it easy."

"That man," she said, "he killed them."

He lowered her nightgown and stood up straight.

"Yes, he did."

"He saved my life," she said. "They were gonna kill me. Where is he?"

"He's in jail."

"Jail? But why?"

"You were in no shape to talk yesterday," the doctor said, "so the sheriff had to put him in a cell until he could figure out what happened."

"B-but he was defending me," she said, "and himself. I have to tell somebody."

"I suspect right now he's talkin' with the judge," the doctor said. "After that they'll probably come and talk to you. You'll have your chance to set things straight."

"The . . . judge?"

"Yes."

She hugged herself, turned away from the doctor.

"I don't wanna talk to the judge."

"Can't say I blame you, Miz Burkett," the doctor said, "but I don't think you're gonna have much of a choice, seein' as how all his sons were killed out at your place."

"Yes," she said, "his sons."

"Miz Burkett—Liz—that man Lancaster, he admitted that he had to kill the other three, but he says he didn't kill your Harry."

"No," she said, "no, he didn't."

"Then who did?"

Without turning back to the doctor she said, "I guess I better save that for the judge."

Chapter Fifteen

"I didn't kill your son Harry, Judge," Lancaster said. "When I reached the house the other three men were dragging Liz Burkett out of the house. They were heading for the well."

"You think they were intending to throw her in?" the judge asked.

"Yes, sir, I do."

"And you tried to stop them."

"I did."

"By killing them?"

"I gave them every chance," Lancaster said. "Especially the youngest one."

"Ben."

"He was the last to draw. I warned him to stop, but he wouldn't."

"You're a professional gunman, Mr. Lancaster," the judge said, "so none of the three of them ever had a chance."

"Judge—"

"Some might call that murder."

"They'd be wrong."

"Did it ever occur to you," the judge asked,

"that my three sons were trying to subdue my son Harry's wife?"

"Subdue her?"

"Perhaps trying to keep her from hurting herself, or them?"

"Judge," Lancaster said, shaking his head, "talk about not having a chance . . ."

"So what you're saying," the judge said, cutting him off, "is that when you got to the house, Harry was already dead. Is that correct?"

"That's the only way I can see that it happened."

"Then who killed him?"

"I don't know," Lancaster said. "I guess you'll have to ask the only witness."

"My daughter-in-law."

"Yes."

Lancaster suddenly had a very uncomfortable feeling. What if Liz Burkett couldn't remember what happened? Or what if she killed her husband and seized this perfect opportunity to blame it on somebody else?

"So I suppose that's what we should do, then," the judge said. "Go over to the Dutchman and talk to Elizabeth."

"Together?"

The judge gave it some thought, then said, "Sure, why not? Any reason why you wouldn't want to see my daughter-in-law again?"

"No reason at all."

But the judge didn't move. He remained seated.

"Mr. Lancaster, have you ever met my daughter-in-law before?"

"No."

"Or my son Harry?"

"No, sir."

"You've never been here before? In Gallows? Around the town?"

"No, sir."

"You're very respectful, aren't you?" the judge said. "For a hired killer."

"Those days are behind me."

"So you say." The judge stood up. "All right, let's get the sheriff and we'll all head over to the Dutchman and have a chat with Elizabeth."

"Suits me," Lancaster said, and stood up.

Chapter Sixteen

Doc Meade was still in Liz Burkett's room when the knock came at the door. He was not surprised to find the three men standing in the hall.

"Doc," the judge said.

"Judge."

"Can we talk with my daughter-in-law?"

"You can, but not for long. She's still a little fuzzy about what happened."

"Thank you."

They stepped into the room, the judge first. As they approached the bed, the judge stepped to one side, the sheriff the other. Lancaster decided to stand at the foot of the bed.

"Elizabeth," the judge said, "it's your father-in-law. I have the sheriff and Mr. Lancaster here with me."

She turned her head away from her father-in-law, as if she didn't want to—or couldn't—look at him, but when she heard Lancaster's name she opened her eyes, searched for him, and then looked at him. She pointed at him, and Lancaster tensed and waited, unsure of what she was going to say.

"He saved me life!" she said. "They were gonna kill me."

"The boys?" the judge asked. "Luke, Tom and Ben?"

"Yes," she said.

"Why, Elizabeth?" the judge asked. "Why did you think the boys were going to kill you?"

"They weren't boys!" she said. "They were men—mean, evil men!"

"Now, Elizabeth," the judge said, "that's not what I asked you. Why did you think they were going to kill you?"

'I didn't think. I knew," she said.

"How?"

"They told me."

"They said they were going to kill you?"

"Yes."

"All right, why?" the judge asked patiently. So patiently, in fact, that Lancaster was surprised. For a man whose sons had been killed, he was remarkably calm. "Why were they going to kill you?" the judge asked.

Liz looked at the sheriff, then at Lancaster. Then she covered her face with both hands and started crying.

"All right," the doctor said, "that's enough for now."

"Not quite, Doctor," the judge said. "We still have not found out who killed Harry."

"Well, you'll have to find out later," the doctor said. "She's in no condition to be interrogated right now."

The two older men faced each other over the bed. The doctor had his chin thrust out. Lancaster sensed a lot of history between these two men, much of it spent glaring at each other.

"All right," the judge said, relenting. "I'll be back later today." He pointed a finger at Meade. "I want answers, Doctor."

"I'm not guaranteeing anything," the doctor said.

The judge held the doctor's eyes a few seconds longer, then turned and left the room. The sheriff gave Lancaster a helpless look, then followed.

"What are you supposed to do?" the doctor asked Lancaster.

"Follow them out, I guess," he said.

"You goin' back to a cell?" the doctor asked.

"Guess I better go and find out," Lancaster said. "If I'm not, I'll come back and see how she is."

"All right."

"Do you have a nurse, or a woman, who can stay with her?" Lancaster asked.

"The women in this town . . . they don't really like her all that much."

"There must be somebody."

The doctor thought a moment, then said, "I think there might be. I'll let you know."

"Thanks, Doc."

Lancaster left the room, got down to the lobby to find the judge and the sheriff in conversation. As he approached them the judge looked at him without any expression on his face, and then left the hotel.

The lawman turned to Lancaster.

"Am I going back to a cell?" Lancaster asked.

"No," Jessup said, "but you can't leave town."

"I'm not ready to leave town," Lancaster said. "I need to buy a horse. By the way, where's my rig?"

"The livery."

"And my gun?"

"Back at the office," Jessup said. "Come with me and I'll give it to you."

"I get my gun back without a fight?"

"Don't be so happy about that," the sheriff said. "I think the judge might be hopin' you'll get yourself killed if we give you your gun back."

"But why?" Lancaster asked. "He knows I had to kill his sons."

"Did you hear how that sounded?" Jessup asked. "You killed three of the man's sons. And he still doesn't know for sure you didn't kill the fourth."

"I get it," Lancaster said. "I'm still better off with my gun than without it, though."

"No argument from me," Jessup said. "Let's go."

Chapter Seventeen

Lancaster stepped from the sheriff's office moments later, feeling a lot less naked now that he had his gun back around his waist.

Now that he'd lost his cell he needed a hotel room, so he returned to the Dutchman Hotel. The desk clerk, who had seen him earlier in the company of the judge and the sheriff, smiled as he approached the desk.

"Yes, sir?"

"I need a room."

"Certainly, sir. If you'll just sign the register?" The clerk turned to collect a key from the wall behind him. When he turned back and read Lancaster's name in the register he hesitated before handing him his key.

"Very good, sir," he said. "You'll be on the second floor, room eleven."

"Thanks."

"Any idea, sir, how long you'll be with us?"

"No."

Lancaster went up to his room, found that he

was down the hall from Liz Burkett. He took a
look at the room, was satisfied with it, and then
left the hotel to go to the livery to collect his saddlebags.

Two men had watched as Lancaster left the sheriff's office. They'd followed him to the hotel and
waited outside, where they picked up a third man.
As Lancaster came out of the hotel, the third man
said, "Hey, he's got his gun."

"So what?" the first man asked.

"Well, he took the Burketts alone, three to one,"
the third man said.

"We can get the drop on him," the second man
suggested.

They watched to see which way Lancaster was
going to walk. It wouldn't do to brace him right
there in front of the hotel. Way too public.

"He looks like he might be headin' for the livery," the first man said. "Let's just trail along behind him and see what he does."

"Suits me," the second man said.

"Me, too."

All three men followed Lancaster, keeping a
good distance behind him.

Lancaster entered the livery, recognized the liveryman from yesterday, when he met the sheriff
there before they rode out to the Burkett place together.

"Lookin' fer yer rig?" the man asked.

"That's right."

"Got it back here."

"I just need the saddlebags," Lancaster said. "I'd appreciate it if you'd keep the saddle here until I can buy a new horse."

"I got some horses out back."

"Good ones?"

"Whaddya wanna do, race 'em?"

"I just don't want it to drop dead after I ride it a mile."

"You can take a look if ya like," the man said. "Come on over to the back door."

He followed the man out the back door to a corral behind the stable. There were six horses, and they all looked pretty worn. He found a six-year-old mare that at least looked sturdy. They talked money, but Lancaster decided not to make a decision right at that moment, so he told the man he'd think about it.

He left the livery carrying his saddlebags, and did not go out the front door. He wasn't looking for trouble, and he knew that the three men following him were, so he took another route, which actually ended up putting him behind the jail.

The three men waiting in front of the livery were getting impatient.

"Where the hell is he?" the first man, Jelly Simms, asked. Simms was friends with Eddie Pratt, who was friends with Deputy Hector Adams.

"We should go in and get 'im," said the second man, Zack Teller.

"You're too impatient," the third man, Winston Hunter, said. "I ain't in a hurry to die."

Robert J. Randisi

"You was friends with Ben Burkett, wasn't ya?" Teller asked.

"Yeah, so? Still don't mean I wanna die."

"Well, I was friends with Luke, and I want this fella," Teller said.

"Then go on in and see what's holdin' him up," Simms said.

"Well," Teller said, backing off, "maybe we can wait a little longer."

Chapter Eighteen

Lancaster took a moment to walk up to the back wall of the jail. He looked down at the ground just beneath the window of the cell he'd spent the night in. There were some clear boot marks there and, as he hunkered down to take a closer look, he could see that the right boot had a hole right where the ball of the foot would be.

He stood and decided to see how far he'd be able to track that boot print. Tossing his saddlebags over his shoulder he followed the trail into the brush, where he quickly lost it. He was not an expert tracker, so there was no way he could track through brush. But if that boot print showed in town anywhere, he'd know it by sight.

He turned, walked back toward the jailhouse. He found a side alley and followed it to the main street.

Simon Bray was the judge's law clerk. He was in his late twenties, and while he thought of himself as a law clerk, the judge treated him as an errand boy.

The judge called Bray into his office when he returned and said, "I want you to send a telegram."

"Yes, sir."

The judge sat at his desk and wrote two lines, handed the folded piece of paper to the younger man.

"Now, sir?"

"Yes, Simon, right now."

"Yes, sir. Should I wait for an answer?"

"No, just tell the key operator to bring the answer to me as soon as it comes in."

"Yes, sir."

Bray practically ran from the man's office.

The judge sat back in his chair and closed his eyes. Four dead sons, but what he was thinking about was his mistress and what they had done the night before.

Of course, he had to do something about his four sons being dead. It was just a matter of saving face. It didn't matter that he hadn't felt particularly close to any of them. Harry was probably the only one who was worth anything, which is why he got him the job as a deputy, hoping that he would eventually become sheriff.

But there was another son that no one in town knew of; Mildred did not even know about him. He was his firstborn by another woman, a woman who was now dead. And it was he whom Simon Bray was sending the telegram to.

There was one son whom the judge was very proud of, and that man would soon be coming to Gallows to save face for his father.

Simon Bray hurried to the telegraph office and handed the message to the key operator.

"From the judge?" the clerk asked.

"Yes."

The operator read the lines on the paper. "This makes no sense." He looked at Bray. "Did you read it?"

"No."

"Why not?"

"It's none of my business."

"Aren't you even curious?"

"No."

"Do you know who this man is?"

Bray shook his head.

"Jesus," the clerk said, shaking his head. "No curiosity."

Chapter Nineteen

When Lancaster got back to the hotel he put his saddlebags in his room, then walked down the hall to Liz Burkett's room. He knocked on the door and was surprised when it was opened by a handsome woman with long red hair and a suspicious look on her face. She had a hard-won beauty that a woman in her early forties earns, a beauty that is only enhanced by a few lines and wrinkles.

"Yes?" she asked.

"My name is Lancaster," he said. "I'm here to check on Liz Burkett's condition."

"Oh yeah," the woman said, "the Doc mentioned your name. Come on in."

He entered, and she closed the door and turned to face him. Now that she knew who he was, though, the suspicious look had not faded, which meant it had not been meant for him, but for all men. Or maybe just for all people.

The room was large so the bed was far enough away from the door that Liz did not yet know he was there. Or maybe she was asleep.

"My name is Rusty Connors," the woman said. "No comments, please."

"I had none to make."

"Most people like to say something about my hair."

"Not me."

She was wearing men's clothes—a cotton shirt, trousers and boots.

"Is Liz awake?"

"I think so," Rusty said. "The Doc just asked me to come up and keep an eye on her."

"He told me the women in town don't like her very much," Lancaster said.

"I don't have any feelings one way or another," Rusty said. "Besides, the women in town don't like me much, either."

"Why's that?"

"We don't know each other well enough to go into that," she said. "Why don't you go and see if Liz is awake?"

"I will, thanks."

He walked to the bed, found Liz lying with her eyes open, her head turned to the right so she could look out the window.

"Liz?"

He stood to the left of the bed, so she had to turn her head to see him.

"Mr. Lancaster?"

"Just Lancaster," he said. "How are you feeling?"

"Truthfully? I feel . . . at peace."

"Because your husband is dead?"

73

She nodded. "Is that horrible of me?"

"Not at all," Lancaster said. "He used to beat you, didn't he?"

"Yes," she said, "all the time."

"Yesterday?"

"Yes," she said. "H-he punched me in the stomach."

"Why?"

"Usually," she said, "he didn't need much of a reason to wail on me, but yesterday . . . yesterday I said I wanted to have a baby."

"So he punched you in the stomach?"

"To show me what would happen if I got pregnant."

"So you killed him?"

She nodded.

"I couldn't take it anymore," she said, tears streaming down her face. "I picked up the shotgun and I . . . I guess I shot him."

"You guess you shot him?"

"I—I still don't remember everything. . . ."

"What about the brothers?" he asked. "Do you remember them?"

"I remember . . . he told me they were coming over. He was going to go hunting with them. It was . . . after he was dead that they got there. When they saw his body they started to . . . to beat me, and drag me outside. They were gonna kill me, Lancaster, but you saved me."

"And got myself in trouble, apparently."

"I'm sorry about that."

"That's not your fault," he said. "It was my decision to step in. I couldn't just stand there and watch them kill you."

"I'm grateful."

"You haven't told your father-in-law yet that you killed Harry."

"You haven't told him?"

"No."

"Or the sheriff?"

"No."

"That's why I'm not in jail, then."

"Surely the judge knows what kind of man his son was," Lancaster said, "that he beat you?"

"Who do you think he learned it from?" she asked.

"The judge?"

She nodded.

"He beat his own wife for years. He probably still does."

"Why wouldn't she leave?" he asked. "Why wouldn't you leave?"

"Nobody leaves the Burketts," she said. "I was told that when I married Harry."

"Told by Harry?"

She shook her head.

"The judge told me."

"Then why did you go through with it?"

"He told me on my wedding night," she said, "when it was too late."

"Well," Lancaster said, "it's over now. Harry's dead."

"It's not over," she said. "The judge will have the sheriff arrest me, and I'll have to go to his court."

"A jury will understand."

"Not in this town," she said. "But then, I might never make it to court."

"Tell me, Liz," Lancaster said, "why don't the women in this town like you?"

"I'm not from here," she said. "Harry and the judge brought me here from back east. That's where the wedding took place."

"So for that reason they don't like you?"

"Harry was the pick of the judge's four sons," she said. "The young ones hate me because he took someone from outside of Gallows as his wife. The old ones hate me because their daughters weren't picked."

"Sounds idiotic to me."

"The judge is more than a judge here," she said. "He's more like . . . a king."

"And I killed three of the princes."

"And I killed the one who was next in line," she said. "Lancaster, neither one of us is gonna leave this town alive."

"We'll see about that, Liz," Lancaster said. "I don't give in that easy."

"I'm not strong," she said, "or I would have left him before this."

"You were strong enough to kill him," Lancaster said.

"I . . . snapped," she said. She turned her face to the window again. "I'm horrible."

"Why do you say that?"

"Because," she said, looking at him again, "I wish I could remember killing him."

Chapter Twenty

As Lancaster backed away from the bed he could literally see Liz Burkett drift off to sleep. The woman was battered, tortured, frightened, guilty and relieved. No wonder she was exhausted.

He turned and saw Rusty Connors looking at him.

"If I married a man and he hit me, I'd kill him when he slept," she said.

"I wouldn't blame you."

"I've got a bottle of whiskey here," she said. "I give her a sip when she gets upset. You want a drink?"

"Sure."

Rusty walked to the table where she had a bottle and two glasses. She poured two fingers of whiskey into each glass and then handed him one.

"Thanks."

She sipped and said, "The poor kid—she's exhausted."

"I know."

"Why did you save her?"

"Like I told her," he answered, "I couldn't just watch them kill her."

"Most men would've ridden on and ignored the situation."

"Is that what you think?"

"It's what I know."

"You haven't had much luck with men, have you?" he said.

"I don't know any women who have."

"Well," he said, "there must be some out there, somewhere."

"Maybe," Rusty said. She raised her glass to him. "Maybe it's you."

"Maybe what's me?" he asked.

She finished her drink and put the empty glass down.

"Maybe you are the first decent man I've ever met," she said.

"Decent?" he asked, laughing softly. "There aren't many who'd describe me that way."

"Maybe once you weren't," she said, "but now you are. Only a decent man would've done what you did for her. Only a decent man would've stayed here afterward. And only a decent man would not mount a horse tomorrow morning and ride out of here, leave her to pay for what she did."

"She didn't do anything that she should have to pay for." He put his empty glass down. "Thanks for the drink."

"Sure," she said. "Come around anytime."

"I'm down the hall," he said "Room eleven. If you need anything."

"Thanks. I'll remember."
He nodded and left.

He stood at the window in his room, looking down at the street. Was Rusty right? Would the old Lancaster mount a horse in the morning and leave? And not care that he might be wanted if he did? Or that he'd be leaving behind a woman who was going to pay for trying to save her own life?

If she went to trial, would a jury of people from this town understand that she was tired of being beaten on by a man she thought loved her?

And why couldn't she remember killing her husband, Harry Burkett?

Was it possible that someone had been there? That someone else had killed Harry Burkett?

Was it possible that Elizabeth Burkett was innocent of her husband's murder?

And if she was, who would try to prove it, if not him?

Chapter Twenty-one

Lancaster was having a beer in the Three Aces Saloon when Sheriff Jessup walked in. The lawman seemed surprised to see him, and joined him at the bar.

"I'm surprised to see you out and about," he said, signaling the bartender for a beer.

"What else was I supposed to do?" Lancaster asked. "Hole up in my room?"

Jessup accepted his beer and looked around the saloon, which was doing its usual brisk business. There were four girls working the room and plenty of games going on at the tables. There was also a stage, but it was quiet at the moment. The only music was coming from a bad piano player— a painfully bad piano player.

"Somebody here is bound to try to take a shot at you," Jessup said.

"Sheriff, you know what I've been able to find out?" Lancaster asked.

"What?"

"The Burkett's were not liked by as many people as you might have thought."

"Really?"

"Now feared, that's another thing," he went on. "But they weren't even feared because of themselves—they were feared because of who their father was."

"I knew that," Jessup said, sipping his beer.

"Well, you didn't tell me."

"I did," the lawman said. "I told you the judge owns this town."

"Okay, so you kind of told me," Lancaster said, "but I don't think I have to watch out at every corner for a friend of the Burkett boys."

"Well," Jessup said, "that decision is yours."

"Has the Judge been back to see Liz yet?" Lancaster asked.

"No," Jessup said. "The last I heard he was gonna wait until tomorrow to see her again. Why?"

"Just wondering."

"Have you seen her again?"

"I happened to get a room down the hall from her, so yes, I stopped in to see her," he said. "She has a woman named Rusty staying with her."

"Yeah, yeah, Rusty Connors," Jessup said, nodding. "That figures."

"Why? Because they're equally disliked by the women in town?"

"Exactly."

"You know, this town doesn't seem like a place I'd like to live," Lancaster said.

"You and me both," Jessup said. "The difference is, you get to leave—maybe."

"Yeah, maybe."

"Did you talk to Liz again?"

"Yeah, I did."

"And did she tell you anything . . . important?" Jessup asked.

"You mean, like anything I'd want to repeat? No. Let the judge get his own information."

"You mean if Liz confessed to you that she killed her husband, you wouldn't tell the judge?"

"No," Lancaster said. "She'd have to tell him that herself."

"And what if she doesn't?" Jessup said. "What if she tells him you killed Harry?"

"I'll deal with that if the time comes."

Jessup finished his beer and set the mug on the bar. He waved the bartender away.

"I've got to make my rounds."

"Why don't you just let your deputy make the rounds? After all, you're the boss."

"I don't have a deputy," Jessup said. "I fired him today."

"Ah."

"By the way," Jessup added, "he blames you for his getting fired and, like we said, he's got kind of an itchy finger, so . . ."

"Ah," Lancaster said, nodding. "Is he any good with his gun?"

"That don't matter," Jessup explained, "because he won't come straight at you. He'll try to shoot you in the back."

"Well, thanks for the warning. By the way, speaking of shooting me in the back, I found something behind the jail."

"Oh? What?"

"A boot print, with a hole in the right one"—he lifted his own foot to show the sheriff the bottom of his boot—"there."

"You know how many men in this town have holes in their boots?"

"Nope," Lancaster said, "but if I spot a print, I'm going to follow it."

Chapter Twenty-two

Simms, Hunter and Teller watched as the sheriff had a beer with Lancaster, and then left.

"That sonofabitch," Simms said. "He got away from us at the livery, but he ain't gettin' away from us here."

"We can't take him in here," Hunter said.

"Very good, stupid," Teller said. "There's too damn many people."

"We should wait for him outside," Hunter said.

"No," Simms said, "that's what we did outside the livery."

"So what do we do this time?" Hunter asked.

"We sit here," Simms said, "and wait for him to leave. Then we follow him out and take him in the street."

"Three against one should be pretty good odds," Teller said.

"There were three Burkett boys against him," Hunter pointed out.

"We'll spread out," Simms said. "He got the boys close together."

"How do you know that?"

"I heard it from Eddie Pratt, who heard it from the deputy," Simms said. "They were all standing over the woman, Harry's wife."

"Was they gonna rape her?" Hunter asked.

"I don't know what they were gonna do," Simms said, "but it don't matter. We're gonna kill him."

"Good," Teller said.

"We need another round," Simms said.

"What if he leaves?" Hunter asked.

"He just ordered another, himself," Simms said.

Hunter looked at Lancaster, who was lifting a new mug of beer to his lips.

"Okay," Hunter said.

They waved for one of the girls.

Lancaster thought he was losing his touch.

He had not spotted the three men until they waved at one of the girls for another round of drinks. They must have been in the saloon already when he got there.

Just because he didn't hire his gun out anymore didn't mean that he could unlearn all the lessons he'd learned over the years. And watching his own back, that was lesson number one.

He decided to let them wait while he finished his second beer. While he was nursing it the batwings opened and ex-deputy Hector Adams came walking in. Or staggering. It was obvious he'd been drinking already.

Lancaster waited to see if the ex-deputy would see him.

Adams stopped just inside the doors and looked

around, missing Lancaster, who was part of the crowd at the bar. He did spot his friend Simms, though, and Simms' two friends.

"Simms!" he shouted, drunkenly staggering toward their table. "How the hell are ya? Buy me a drink?"

Simms saw Hector staggering toward them and told his friends, "Grab him before he attracts too damn much attention."

"What do we do with him?" Hunter asked.

"Sit him down," Simms said. "We'll give him a drink. That should shut him up."

Hunter and Teller stood up, quickly grabbed Hector and sat him down.

"Whoa!" Hector said as his butt hit the chair. "Nice to see you, too, buddy. Got a drink?"

"Sure," Simms said, waving to a girl. "Beer?"

"Whiskey!" Hector snapped. "What the hell do I want with beer?"

"Whiskey," Simms told the girls. "A bottle and one glass."

The pretty blonde smiled and said, "Sure thing, honey."

"Pretty girl," Hector said, staring after the girl owlishly. "Both of them."

"Man, is he drunk," Teller said.

Simms leaned over and said, "We got to keep him from seein' Lancaster at the bar. He might ruin our whole damn plan."

"And get us killed," Teller said.

The girl came back with the whiskey and four glasses.

"One glass, girl," Simms said to her. "We're gonna stick with beer."

"Whatever you say, sugar."

Simms opened the bottle and pushed it and the glass toward Hector.

"There ya go, Hector."

"You're a good man, Jelly," Hector Adams said, "A good man."

He eschewed the glass and lifted the bottle to his lips.

Chapter Twenty-three

Lancaster knew what he would have done in the old days. Walked right up to the table and challenged the men—three or four. And he wouldn't have worried about innocent bystanders being hurt.

Since he wouldn't—or couldn't—do that, he had two other options. Wait until they followed him out and face them in the street or leave quickly and lose them. If he did the latter, though, he'd probably just be putting off the inevitable.

Maybe, he thought, what he should do was combine the old Lancaster with the new.

Yeah, that wasn't a bad idea.

He grabbed his half mug of beer from the bar, turned and walked through the crowded saloon to the table the four men were sharing. One of them saw him coming, and his eyes got wide.

"What the—" the man said as Lancaster reached them. The other two looked up at him in surprise. The ex-deputy was too involved with his bottle to notice.

"Hello, gents."

Hector Adams put his bottle down and squinted across the table at Lancaster.

"Who's this?" he asked. "A new frien'?"

"That's right," Lancaster said, "I'm a new friend to all of you, so I'm going to give you some advice."

"Why would we need advice from you, Mister?" Simms asked. "We don't even know you."

"Sure you do," Lancaster said. "The deputy here—well, ex-deputy—he knows me."

"I do?"

"And you three, you followed me to the livery stable today, probably meant to brace me when I came out—only I never came out, right?"

"We don't know—" Teller started.

"Yeah, yeah, you don't know who I am," Lancaster said. "Look, let me give you the advice and then I'll be on my way."

"What advice?" Hunter asked.

"You friends of the Burkett boys—you were all friends with them, right? One or all of them?"

"So?" Teller asked.

"Well, forget about getting revenge for them," Lancaster said. "If you follow me again I'm through talking. Get it? If I see you again I'm not going to have any choice but to kill you. Each of you."

"Kill you," Hector said, and started to giggle.

"Mister—" Simms started, but Lancaster stopped them with a raised hand.

"This was just some advice, gents. But remember,

89

all these people here saw us together tonight. If I show up dead with a bulletin in my back, the law's going to come looking for you."

"The law," Hector said, chucking, "lookin' for all of you."

"Think about it," Lancaster said.

As he started away, Simms said, "I thought you were supposed to be some hotshot killer. You couldn't just face us in the street? You had ta do this?"

"Consider that I may have saved your lives," Lancaster said.

"Or yours," Teller said petulantly.

"Look, if you guys want to face me in the street come on, but let's do it one at a time. How's that?"

The three men looked at one another, then away.

"No? None of you? Okay, then. Think about my offer. Stay away from me and live. Come after me and . . . well, you get the idea."

Lancaster turned and walked back to the bar, left the empty mug there and left.

As Lancaster went out the batwing doors Hunter asked, "Do we go after him?"

"Are you stupid?" Simms asked. "You heard what he said. Everybody here saw him with us."

"So?" Hunter asked. "We wasn't gonna shoot him in the back, was we? I thought we was gonna face him in the street."

"We were gonna shoot him down in the street," Teller said. "Jesus, you are stupid."

"Who's stupid?" Hector asked. "Shoot who in the street?"

"Lancaster," Hunter said.

"Lancaster?" Hector sat up straight. "Where is that sumbitch? I'll put a bullet in him!"

"He just left, stupid," Hunter said, taking the opportunity to call somebody else stupid.

"Where'd he go?" Hector demanded. "I'll blow a hole in him."

Simms, making a quick decision, grabbed Hector by the shoulders, pulled him to his feet and said, "Come on!"

The others followed.

Chapter Twenty-four

Lancaster was walking back to his hotel when the first shot came. The bullet went wide as he dropped into a crouch and turned. There was a man standing about twenty feet behind him, legs spread, gun in hand.

"That you, Lancaster?" a voice called. "I can't see ya. Come closer."

Hector Adams, the ex-deputy. Of the four men seated at that table, he was the last one Lancaster expected to come after him. He was too drunk.

"Come on, Lancaster. Step into the light."

"Deputy, you don't want to do—"

"I ain't a deputy no more!" Hector shouted. "That's because of you."

"What makes you think I had anything to do with you losing your job? I heard you got fired for being drunk . . . like you are now."

"Before you came to town I had a job," Hector Adams said. "After you got here, I got fired. I ain't stupid, ya know."

"You could've fooled me. This seems real stupid

to me. Trying to shoot me in the back while you're drunk."

"Front, back, I don't care. Let's do it."

Hector fired again, missed by a wide margin. Lancaster heard glass break.

"Hector—"

He fired again. Came close enough for Lancaster to flinch. He drew his gun.

"Don't make me fire my gun, Hector," Lancaster said. "Your friends put you up to this. It's not a good idea."

"Damn you, Lancaster. If you won't come to me I'll come to you."

He started walking toward Lancaster, who knew the closer he got, the better chance he had of hitting him.

"Damn it, Hector."

The ex-deputy raised his gun again, and Lancaster had no choice. He fired once, trying to hit Hector someplace that wouldn't be fatal. The bullet struck the man in the left hip, spun him around and put him down. He screamed in pain, but was still trying to raise his gun for a shot. Lancaster figured if Hector wasn't so drunk, the pain would have been less bearable. He moved quickly, before Hector could bring the gun to bear, and kicked it out of the ex-deputy's hand.

"Damn it, Hector," Lancaster said, looking down at the man.

Hector looked up at him.

"Ow!"

Lancaster stayed where he was while the saloon emptied out. Men began shouting, running in all directions. A few of them spotted him and the fallen Hector and came over.

"What happened here?" someone asked.

"Hey, is that Hector?" another asked.

"Ain't that the man who shot the Burkett boys?" a third shouted.

"This man got drunk and started shooting at me," Lancaster said. "I warned him and then fired back. Would someone go and get the doctor?"

"He ain't dead?" someone asked.

Hector was rolling around on the ground, moaning in pain.

"What do you think?" Lancaster asked.

"Somebody should take this man's gun?" a voice said.

"Anybody want to try?" Lancaster countered.

It got quiet and tense while more men came over. A few more minutes and somebody might have gotten brave, but at that moment a loud voice called out.

"Okay, okay, that's all, folks," Sheriff Jessup said. "Break it up. Go back to the saloon, or go home."

"He shot your deputy, Sheriff," somebody yelled. "Ain't you gonna do nothin' about it?"

"Hector's not a deputy anymore," Jessup said. "So don't try to tell me how to do my job. Now break it up!"

Jessup came over to Lancaster.

"Tell me what happened?"

"Your boy got drunk, took a few shots at me.

Got a broken window someplace behind me to prove it. I took one shot to try to stop him."

"Doesn't surprise me," Jessup said. "Where'd he see you?"

"In the saloon, where you left me," Lancaster said. "He was sitting with three other men who have been following me all day."

"Who?"

"I don't know their names, but I can point them out. I went over and talked with them so that everybody would see us together. Told them if I turned up dead you'd be looking for them."

"Why'd you do that?"

"So I wouldn't have to kill them, Sheriff. I did what I could to avoid it. I also warned Hector here about three times before I had to fire."

"He was too drunk to hit you."

"He started coming closer," Lancaster said. "He could've hit me by accident."

Hector was still rolling around on the ground, leaving a blood trail.

"Where'd you hit him?"

"The left hip. I told somebody to go get the doc."

As if on cue, Doc Meade showed up, carrying his black bag.

"Doc, see how bad Hector's hurt, will ya?" Jessup asked.

"Sure thing."

He crouched down and examined the wounded man.

"He's hit in the hip. Not too bad. Can we get some boys to carry him to my office?"

"Sure," Jessup said, looking around at the few stragglers who were still around. He picked out three, and they lifted Hector and carried him away.

"You hit?" the doc asked Lancaster.

"No, I'm fine, thanks. Did you check on Liz Burkett tonight?"

"Yeah, she's okay. Her memory seems to be comin' back, but she still can't remember actually shootin' Harry."

"You think she's tellin' the truth?" Jessup asked.

The doctor looked at him. "You think she's lyin', trying to set up a defense for herself?"

"Maybe she's gonna blame Lancaster," Sheriff Jessup said.

"I don't think so," the older man said.

"Why not?"

"She's a decent woman, Sheriff."

"Decent woman who might be going on trial for murder," the lawman said. "You better go take care of your new patient, Doc."

Meade followed the men who had been carrying Hector Adams.

"You better come to my office," Jessup said.

"What for? Aw, you're not going to put me back in a cell, are you?"

Jessup studied him for a moment, then said, "What the hell. Show me where this broken window is."

"Sounded like it came from somewhere back here . . ." Lancaster said, leading the way.

Chapter Twenty-five

Lancaster decided to go back to Jessup's office with him, after all. Jessup opened a bottle of whiskey and poured some into two coffee cups. They sat on either side of his desk.

"I think those other three men took advantage of Hector being drunk and sent him after me."

"To accomplish what?"

"Well, either he'd kill me or I'd kill him," Lancaster said. "If they didn't know you fired him, maybe they thought I'd get into trouble for shooting, or killing, a lawman."

"You said they've been followin' you all day?" Jessup asked.

"Followed me to the livery, waited for me outside. I avoided them by going out the back."

The sheriff sat back in his chair and stared at Lancaster.

"What?"

"You really are tryin' to avoid killin' anybody, aren't you?" he asked. "I mean, you could've killed Hector if you wanted to."

"I don't want to kill anyone, Sheriff," Lancaster said. "I never did want to."

"But you used to get paid to do it."

"That didn't mean I wanted to," Lancaster explained. "I made a living doing it. I was good at it."

"I've never met a reformed killer before," Jessup said.

"As a lawman," Lancaster said, "you probably never thought the reformed killer existed."

"I never thought about it much," Jessup said. "I just figured a lawman is a lawman, and a killer is a killer."

"And I'm not either."

Jessup stared at Lancaster again for a period of time, his expression quizzical.

"What are you thinking now?" Lancaster asked.

"You could be."

"I could be what?"

"A lawman," Jessup said. "You could be my new deputy."

"And what would the judge have to say about that?" Lancaster asked.

"I don't know," Jessup said. "Maybe he'll think I've lost my mind and fire me."

"Is that it?" Lancaster asked. "You want to get fired?"

"I don't want to," Jessup said, "but maybe it wouldn't be the worst thing to happen to me."

"I guess that's going to be between you and the judge."

Jessup poured them another drink each and sat back, putting his feet up on his desk.

"I gotta tell you, I think tonight was just the beginning," he said to Lancaster.

"I thought we went over this," Lancaster said. "Your boy was drunk. I think I've got those others three talked out of trying me."

"There'll be more," Jessup said. "If I was you I think I'd just leave town."

"You know, despite what I used to do for a living," Lancaster said, "I've never been wanted, and I don't want to start now. If I left, the judge would put a poster out on me—probably dead or alive."

"You're most likely right."

"When is he going to make a decision about what to do about all this?"

"After he talks with Liz again, I guess."

"And if she clears me?"

"She can't clear you of killing three of them, only Harry."

"The shooting of the three was justified," Lancaster said.

"I think the judge will decide that."

"If he tries to railroad me, he's going to find it hard to do."

"Ah," Jessup said, "there's the old Lancaster."

"I don't have to revert to being the old Lancaster to defend myself," he said.

"Just remember you're all alone in this town," Jessup said.

"What about you?"

"What about me?"

"What side are you on?"

"I'm on my side, Lancaster," Jessup said. "Don't forget that I'm the sheriff here—I work here. Just because I don't like the judge, or because I'm havin' a drink with you, or because I warned you, doesn't mean I'm gonna go against him."

Lancaster leaned forward and set the coffee cup on the sheriff's desk.

"Thanks for clearing that up for me, Sheriff."

"I'm just makin' my position clear."

"Don't worry, it's clear," Lancaster said. "Now let me make mine clear. You already know that just because I don't want to kill anyone doesn't mean I won't to defend myself."

"I got that."

"Good."

Lancaster stood up. "You're sending out mixed signals, Sheriff," Lancaster said.

"I thought I made myself clear."

"I think you might be playing a game of your own. You should know I don't like to play games."

"Are you threatening me?"

"Now, why would I want to threaten the only friend I have in town?"

Jessup sat forward. "Don't go tellin' anyone in town that we're friends," he warned.

"I wouldn't do that, Sheriff," Lancaster said. "Somebody might take a shot at you instead of me if they thought that."

"Look, I been tryin' to be straight with you, Lancaster," Jessup said.

"Yeah, well, your straight is starting to seem a little crooked to me," Lancaster said, heading for the door.

Chapter Twenty-six

Lancaster went right back to his hotel after leaving the sheriff's office. He was sure he had no friends in town. Not one. The sheriff had his own agenda going. He didn't know what it was yet, but he knew he didn't trust the man.

Sheriff Jessup had another drink after Lancaster left. He wondered whether he'd made a mistake. Lancaster had seemed like someone who might help him out, if he played him right. But maybe he hadn't, and maybe now he'd blown his chance.

Tomorrow the judge would talk to his daughter-in-law, and they'd all find out what kind of story they were working with. So he wouldn't know until then whether he could still use Lancaster. Too bad he hadn't killed Hector. That might have made things a lot more black-and-white.

The doctor removed the bullet from Hector Davis' hip without much trouble. He was glad the ex-deputy was drunk; it was almost as if he had self medicated himself against the pain.

In fact, the whiskey fumes coming from the man's mouth were almost making the doctor's eyes tear.

"Doc?" Hector asked.

"Yeah?"

"What am I doin' here?"

"You're here because you're a stupid, stupid man, Hector."

"Really?" Hector said. "You got medicine for that?"

"Unfortunately, that's not somethin' I can cure, son."

"Too bad," Hector said, and passed out.

Doc Meade bandaged the man and then left him to sleep it off in the examination room.

It would have been very easy for a man like Lancaster to kill Hector. The fact that he'd chosen to only wound him indicated that he had, indeed, left his old life behind him.

Meade wasn't sure that was such a good thing. The town of Gallows probably could have used the man Lancaster used to be—but maybe they could still use the Lancaster they got.

In the saloon Simms, Hunter and Teller were back at their table.

"Well, that didn't work, and Hector almost got killed," Teller said.

"And it put Lancaster on his guard," Hunter said.

"You don't think he was on his guard already?" Simms asked. "He spotted us following him to the livery, didn't he?"

"Then why didn't he come out and face us?" Hunter asked.

"I don't know," Simms said, "maybe he's lost his bottle."

"Didn't seem like he lost nothin' when he came over and talked with us," Hunter said.

"That might've been a bluff," Simms said. "Yeah, that's it. He was bluffin', tryin' to get us to forget about bracing him."

"So you're sayin' he's scared?" Hunter said.

"That's what I'm sayin'," Simms said, as if it were a revelation. "He's scared."

"So," Teller asked, "what do we do now?"

"Nothin' tonight," Simms said, "but tomorrow we'll make our move."

As Lancaster walked past Liz Burkett's door he thought about stopping in, but he didn't want to put any more pressure on the woman. She'd been through enough. He was fairly certain she would tell the judge the same thing she told him about her husband's death. He just hoped the conversation would take place first thing in the morning so he could find out where he stood.

He also wondered whether Rusty Connors was still in the room with Liz, but finding out would have been a silly reason to knock on the door.

He continued to his own room and entered. He took off his gun belt and boots and sat on the bed.

Then, before he could fall asleep, he got up, took the pitcher and basin from the dresser top and put them on the windowsill, where anyone trying to get into the room would have to knock them over. Then he grabbed the wooden chair and jammed the straight back underneath the doorknob. No point in taking any chances. If Hector was stupid enough to try him, who knew how many other drunken, stupid opportunists there were in town?

Chapter Twenty-seven

Sheriff Jessup wasn't married, so he didn't always go home at night. He woke up the next morning in his office, poured some water from a pitcher into a basin and washed his face. He made a pot of coffee, was drinking a second cup when the door to his office opened and the judge stepped in.

"Sheriff."

"Judge. Coffee?"

"No, thanks," the judge said. "I've had your coffee. You ready to go? I want to talk to Elizabeth and get her full story today."

"Yeah, I'm ready," Jessup said.

"Where's Lancaster?"

"Stayin' at the hotel."

"The Dutchman?"

"Yeah."

"Sheriff," the judge said, "are we going to have a problem if I tell you to arrest Lancaster?"

"A problem?" Jessup asked. "We'll have a problem with Lancaster, yeah."

"I mean will you have a problem doing your job," the judge said.

"No, Judge," Jessup said, "I'm up to doin' my job, but I don't have any deputies. I wouldn't have anyone to back my play."

"Don't worry about that," the judge said. "I've taken care of that."

"Really? You hired a deputy?"

"I sent for some help," the judge said. "Should be arriving today."

"Who's that?"

"You'll see," the Judge said. "Come on, I want to get this over with."

"Sure."

They started for the door.

Once outside, the judge stopped and raised a finger to Jessup.

"One more thing," he said.

"What?"

"If it turns out that bitch killed my son herself," the judge said, "I want her ass in a cell, no matter what the doctor says. Understand?"

"I understand, Judge."

Lancaster woke the next day to the fervent hope that this would be his last day in the town of Gallows. For one thing, that wasn't a very comforting name for a town.

He opened the door to his room so he could hear if someone was walking down the hall. As he was pulling his boots on he heard voices and footsteps. He grabbed his gun belt and stepped into the hall just as the judge and the sheriff knocked on Liz's door.

"Mornin', gents," he said, walking toward them. "Mind if I tag along?"

Jessup didn't answer. He looked at the judge.

"No problem, Mr. Lancaster," the judge said, "but I'd like to do the talking."

"Sure," Lancaster said.

The door was opened by Doctor Meade.

"Mornin', Doc," the judge said.

"Mornin', gents," Doc Meade said.

"Can we talk to her this morning?" the judge asked.

"Sure," the doc said. "She's better this mornin'."

"Better, how?" the judge asked.

"She says she remembers," the doc said. "Everythin'."

"That's good news," the judge said.

As they walked into the room, Lancaster was hoping so.

Chapter Twenty-eight

All three men stepped into the room and the doctor stopped them right there.

"I would prefer it if the three of you didn't surround the bed," he said. "Two of you can wait right here. You'll still be able to hear what she says."

"I'll speak to her," the judge said.

The doctor walked the judge to the bed.

"Elizabeth? It's your father-in-law."

Her head was turned toward the window. She turned it back to look at him.

"I did it," she said.

"What?"

"I shot Harry."

"Wha—why did you shoot him?"

"Because he hit me for the last time," she said. "I was fed up. I snapped. I grabbed the shotgun and I shot him."

"You blew his head off, Elizabeth," the judge said.

"That was the only way I could be sure he wouldn't hit me again."

"Let me get this straight," the judge said. "You shot my son because he hit you?"

"Yes."

The judge looked at Meade, then over to where Jessup and Lancaster were standing.

"That's ludicrous," he said to the room. Then he looked at Liz. "You were his wife."

"Does that mean he could hit me anytime he wanted?" she asked.

"Well . . . he was your husband," the judge said, as if that answered the question.

She turned her head away, stared out the window again.

"Doctor, is she sound? Healthy?"

"Reasonably," the doctor said "She still has some bruises—"

"Sheriff," the judge said, "do your duty."

"What?" Lancaster said.

"Liz Burkett," Jessup said, approaching the bed, "you're under arrest. Get up and get dressed."

"Hey," Lancaster said, "this is crazy."

"Judge," the doctor said, "my patient—"

"You just told me she was healthy."

"Yes, but—"

"She just confessed to killing my son," the judge said. "I want her in a cell."

"You're crazy—"

The judge pointed a finger at Lancaster.

"She's the only witness you have that you justifiably shot my other three sons," the judge said. "So things may not be looking good for you in the near future."

110

"You're honestly going to take her to trial for killing a husband who beat her constantly?"

"If he hit her—and what husband doesn't hit his wife when she deserves it—that doesn't justify her killing him," the judge said.

Lancaster stared at the judge, who looked over to the doctor for support, but found another stare.

"Are you married?" he asked Lancaster.

"No."

"Have you ever been?"

"No."

"You, Doc?"

"No."

He looked at the sheriff, who shook his head.

"Then none of you are qualified to judge," he said.

"Gentlemen," the doctor said, "if you will all step out into the hall I'll help my patient get dressed."

They all stepped into the hall.

"I'm not having the sheriff put you in a cell, Lancaster," the judge said. "You better look around for something, or someone, to prove you justifiably killed my sons."

"There was no one else there, judge," Lancaster said. "How am I supposed to do that? You said yourself, your daughter-in-law is my only witness."

"And as soon as she is convicted of killing my son she won't be a very creditable one, will she?" He looked at the sheriff. "I'm not going to wait here. You put that girl in a cell. I'll stop by later."

Robert J. Randisi

He gave Lancaster a look, and then marched down the hall to the stairs.

"He's crazy," Lancaster said.

"He might be, but you heard her confess as well as I did. She killed him."

"In self-defense."

"Well, the exact circumstances haven't come out, yet," Jessup said. "I guess that'll happen in court."

"Sheriff—"

"You still want to help this girl?" Jessup asked.

"Yes."

"Then get her a lawyer who'll defend her," the lawman said, "and good luck finding one in this town."

Chapter Twenty-nine

When the judge entered the office there was a man sitting at his desk. He wore a black hat, black shirt, and maroon leather vest. The judge had no doubt that his trousers and boots were black.

"The vest," he said, closing his door. "Don't tell me you've acquired style."

"Would that be somethin' I got from you, Daddy?" the man asked. "Or from Mummy?"

"Your mother had the taste of a street whore," the judge said.

"My mother was a street whore," the younger man said. "Remember?"

"That was so long ago, Vin." The judge walked to his desk. "Do you mind?"

"Not at all, Papa," Vin said, standing.

"Ah," the judge said, when he saw that his oldest son was now wearing a leather gun belt dyed maroon, "you *have* acquired style. Why not some silver bullets? They would really stand out."

"Silver bullets," Vin said, "would be tacky."

He sat in a chair across from the judge.

"You're looking good, boy."

"I'm forty-four years old," Vin said. "You're the only one who ever calls me *boy*."

"I was hardly a boy myself when you were born."

"Hence the fact my mother was a street whore."

"What are you complaining about?" the judge asked. "You've made a lot of money from me since you tracked me down ten years ago."

"And is that why I'm here today?" Vin asked. He took the telegram from his pocket and read from it. " 'Require your presence immediately. Waste no time.' Very cryptic."

"Well," the judge said, "you didn't waste any time."

"I live in a town fifty miles away," Vin said. "Where you set me up, remember?"

"It was better that way," the judge said. "You know that."

"No, I know that you wanted it that way," Vin said. "Your own private gunman on call at a moment's—or a day's—notice."

"And you've done very well for yourself, boy."

"And so what can I do for you this time, Papa?"

The judge noticed that Vin's hatband was also maroon.

"Your half brothers," the judge said, "are all dead."

"Tsk, tsk," Vin said. "Have I been invited to the funeral? Oh, I'm sorry. Funerals. After never having been invited to the house?"

"No funerals," the judge said. "They haven't been buried yet, but that's neither here nor there."

"How were they killed?" Vin asked. "I mean, I assume they were all killed? They didn't all just . . . drop dead of the same disease?"

"No, indeed," the judge said. "They were all killed—three of them by the same man."

"And the fourth?"

"That would be Harry."

"Ah, your pride and joy."

"You are my pride and joy, boy."

"And how did poor Harry meet his maker?" Vin asked his father.

"He was apparently killed," the judge said, "by his wife."

Vin stared at his father for a few moments, then started laughing.

"You find that funny?"

"I find that hilarious," Vin said. "Was he hitting her? Did she get fed up?"

"Don't you start," the judge said. "There's nothing wrong with a man hitting his own wife. She expects it."

"So you say," Vin said. "How does dear old stepmum feel about that?"

The judge stared across the desk at his son.

"Do you still hate me," he asked, "even after all this time?"

"Hate doesn't go away," Vin said. "Love might. In fact, love does, but not hate. It's so much . . . stronger, don't you think?"

The judge didn't know. He'd never felt either until he met this man, his son by an anonymous street whore he'd been with years ago in San Francisco.

How the boy had tracked him down, he still did not know, but he chose to believe it when Vin told him that he was his father. He had more sand than the other buys put together.

"If you say so," he replied.

"That's right," Vin said. "The judge never feels any emotions, does he?"

The judge just stared at him.

"Do you have any feelings, at all?" Vin asked. "Pain? Do you feel hunger? Thirst?"

"Of course I feel hunger and thirst."

"Well, good," Vin said. "At least that means you're human . . . a little."

"Can we get down to business?" the judge asked.

"Ah, business," Vin said. "At last. Why am I here, Papa?"

"You're here," the judge said, "for vengeance."

Chapter Thirty

Lancaster walked with Liz Burkett and Sheriff Jessup to the jail. Apparently Rusty Connors had brought something for Liz to change into, for she wasn't wearing her bloody dress. Along the way people stopped and stared. Some—men and women—yelled epithets at Liz, who cringed as if the words were stones.

When they got to the jail Jessup put her in the one cell where it would be difficult to shoot her from a window. He'd learned his lesson with Lancaster.

"By the way," Lancaster said, when they were in the office and she was in a cell, "you ever find out whose gun that was?"

"No," Jessup said, "it's still in my desk drawer."

"Mind if I go in and talk to her?"

"No, go ahead," Jessup said. "Just don't try breakin' her out."

"I didn't even try breaking myself out," Lancaster said. "Why would I break her out."

He didn't wait for an answer.

He entered the cellblock and walked to her cell. She was lying curled up on her bunk.

"Liz?"

She didn't answer.

"Liz, we need to talk."

"About what?" she asked without moving.

"About what you told your father-in-law."

She hesitated, then wiped her face and asked, "What do you care? You're free now. I've cleared you of killing my husband."

"That's just it," Lancaster said. "I'm not cleared of killing the other three."

"But I told the judge you did it to save me. You did it in self defense."

"I know you told him that," he said, "but once you admitted to killing your husband, you damaged your credibility as a witness for me."

"What?"

She sat up and stared at him.

"That's not fair."

"Well, I get the feeling that your father-in-law the judge is not a very fair man."

"So . . . what will happen now?"

"You'll go on trial," he said. "If you're convicted, I'll probably go on trial right after you."

"Why doesn't he just kill us?" she asked.

"He can't do that," Lancaster said. "He's a judge. He has to make it look legal."

She covered her face with her hands.

"Liz, did you tell the judge the truth?" Lancaster asked. "Do you remember shooting Harry?"

She removed her hands and stared at him.

118

"Not really," she said, "but I must have."

"It's not as simple as that, Liz," Lancaster said. "We have to be sure."

"My memory," she said, "I just can't . . ."

"We'll have to do something to jog your memory before the trial."

"But what?" she asked.

"I'll have a talk with the doctor and see what he can come up with. Meanwhile, you should be safe here."

"Safe?"

"Just don't worry," he said. "Rest. I'll think of something that will get us both out of this."

"B-but . . . if I didn't kill Harry, who did?" she asked.

"Now, that's a very good question."

"Lancaster?" Vin asked the judge.

"Yes."

"I know that name."

"Apparently he once had a reputation as a hired killer."

"Yeah, I do know the name," Vin said. "He disappeared for a while, and when he resurfaced he was out of the business."

"Well, he's here, and he's making trouble."

"For you, Papa?"

"For the whole town."

"Your town."

"Yes."

"Well," Vin said, "we can't have that. You want me to kill him?"

"I want you to be here," the judge said, "ready to kill him when I say."

"And is it all right if I meet him while I'm waiting?" Vin asked.

"Why not?" the judge said. "You might as well get acquainted with the man who killed three of your brothers."

"Half brothers," Vin reminded his father, "and no loss to anyone, if you ask me."

The judge hadn't asked him, but did agree with him.

Chapter Thirty-one

Lancaster came out of the cellblock, found Jessup behind his desk.

"What's next?" the sheriff asked.

"I don't know," Lancaster lied, because he did not trust the lawman. "I'm just going to . . . walk for now and try to think of something."

"Well," Jessup said, "I'll be here. Let me know what you come up with."

"Yeah, sure," Lancaster said. "Tell me, how quickly can the judge get a jury together to put her on trial?"

"Days, I suppose."

"Hours?"

"Not if he really wants it to look legal," Jessup said. "If he didn't care how it looked, he'd just convene his court and hear the case himself, without a jury."

"Can he do that?"

"He's the judge," Jessup said. "He can do anything he wants."

* * *

Lancaster went directly to the doctor's office, found him tending to a small boy who had apparently hurt his arm. The boy's mother was crying, but the doctor assured her that her boy would be fine.

After the woman left with her son the doctor turned to Lancaster.

"What do you need, Mr. Lancaster?"

"Advice, Doc," Lancaster said, "and help."

"Advice and help about what?"

"Liz Burkett. I don't think she really killed her husband."

"But she confessed," the doctor said. "We all heard her."

"She told me in her cell that she still doesn't remember doing it. She thought confessing would help me, and it's only made things worse for both of us."

"Oh my."

"Can you tell me what to do to jog her memory?" Lancaster asked.

The doctor sat at his desk, took off his wire-framed glasses and rubbed his eyes.

"We know so little about the human mind, Lancaster," he said. "With this kind of memory loss we've only ever been able to do one thing."

"And what's that?"

"Wait."

"We don't have time to wait," Lancaster said. "The judge might convene his court in days, or hours. Advise me, Doctor. Isn't there something you can think of that might jog her memory?"

"Well . . . one possibility might be to take her back there. Back to the scene where it happened. That might jog her memory."

"I don't know if she wants to go back there."

"Well, if you're serious about this, that shouldn't matter," the doctor said. "You should just take her back there."

"Force her?" Lancaster asked. "Could that do any damage to her?"

"I don't know," the doctor said. "Anything's possible, I guess."

"Tell me about the judge," Lancaster asked. "I get the feeling he doesn't really care that his sons have been killed. As a father, I mean."

"I've known the judge for a long time," Doc Meade said. "I've never seen a display of emotion from him that had anything to do with his family. I've never seen him display love or pride in his wife or any of his sons."

"Why is he doing this, then?" Lancaster asked. "Is he just upholding the law?"

"The law doesn't mean a thing to him," the doctor said. "It's all about image for him. His sons have been killed. He can't just let that go. That's an affront to him as a man."

"So it's all about ego?"

"Very much so."

"Thanks, Doc," Lancaster said, "Thanks for talking to me."

"What are you gonna do?"

"I'm going to take her out there," Lancaster

said, "and make her face the moment. Hopefully she'll remember what actually happened."

"But . . . how are you gonna get her out of jail?" the doctor asked.

"Well," Lancaster said, "I sort of promised not to, but I may just have to break her out."

Chapter Thirty-two

Lancaster had not had breakfast, and his stomach was reminding him of that fact. He went back to the Dutchman to eat in their dining room. The people eating there were mostly guests, not townspeople, so they didn't pay much attention to him as he sat alone and ate—except for one man.

The man was dressed all in black except for a maroon vest, hat band and gun belt. He was sitting alone eating breakfast, but he kept watching Lancaster. He didn't know the man, knew that he had never met him or even seen him before, but nevertheless he thought he knew him—or knew the type of man he was.

He felt as if the man was measuring him, in advance of possibly trying him. That kind of thing used to happen all the time, before he changed his lifestyle. But he was sure there were still men out there who didn't care what kind of life he was leading now; they'd just see Lancaster the gunman, a reputation waiting for them to snatch for themselves.

On top of everything else that was going on in

Gallows, now he was going to have to watch his back for this man—although he felt fairly sure this was the kind of man who would come straight at him, face-to-face.

He was having another cup of coffee after finishing his meal when the man surprised him by getting up and walking over to him, carrying his own cup.

"I've been trying to get the waiter to bring me some more coffee," the man said. "I notice you have a pot. Mind if I join you?"

"Sure," Lancaster said. "Help yourself."

The man pulled out the chair across from him, sat down and poured himself some coffee from Lancaster's pot.

"Thanks. You passin' through?"

"That's right."

"Me, too," the man said. He sipped his coffee, then said, "I know you, don't I?"

"Don't think we've ever met," Lancaster said. "I'd remember."

"No, we haven't met," the man said, "but I know you anyway." He put his cup down and extended his right hand—his gun hand. "Name's Vincent Noble."

"Lancaster."

They shook hands.

"Yeah, I thought I recognized you," Vincent said. "You used to have a rep with a gun till you disappeared a few years back."

"More than a few."

"You're right," Vincent said, picking up his cup again. "You reappeared a few years back."

"That's right."

"Not making your way with a gun anymore?"

"No."

"Men like you—with a rep, I mean—don't usually get to walk away from them."

"I'm trying."

"Having any luck?"

"Not as much as I like."

The man nodded.

"What's your business?"

Vincent shrugged. "Same as yours used to be."

"Is that what brings you to town?" Lancaster asked.

"I said I was passing through."

"I know what you said, Vincent," Lancaster said.

Vincent smiled. "Do you want to know if I'm here for you? If I was would I come and sit down with you and warn you?"

"A little scouting trip never hurts," Lancaster commented.

"You're right about that."

"So?"

Vincent smiled. "Would you believe me if I told you no?"

"Probably not."

Vincent shrugged. "Then what's the point of answering?" He finished his coffee and stood up. "Thanks for sharing," he said.

"Yeah," Lancaster said, "you, too."

He had no doubt that Vincent Noble was there for him, but the question was, who hired him? Of course Vincent could have just been passing through and, at breakfast, recognized Lancaster. But Lancaster didn't really think his reputation, such as it was, was worth very much these days.

He finished his coffee, paid his check and left the hotel. He was going to go in search of the name and address Doc Meade had given him for a lawyer—hopefully a lawyer who wouldn't mind going against the judge.

Chapter Thirty-three

The law office he was looking for turned out to be located over a hardware store. The shingle hanging on the side wall was missing some letters, so that instead of saying MIKE DELANEY, it said IKE DELAN Y, ATTORNEY-AT-LAW.

Lancaster had to go around to the side of the building and up a set of rickety wooden stairs to get to the entrance to the office. He knocked and entered when someone shouted for him to do so.

There was no outer office, just one small room. He saw a tall, thick-set man with broad shoulders wearing a white shirt with the sleeves rolled up. He was in the process of moving an oak desk across the floor, and was doing it fairly easily.

"Be right with you," the man said.

"Do you have any idea when the lawyer will be back?" Lancaster asked. "Mike Delaney?"

The man straightened and looked at Lancaster. He could have been on either side of thirty, with curly black hair on his head and forearms.

"I'm Mike Delaney, the lawyer," he said, putting his hand out.

"Oh," Lancaster said, shaking his hand, "sorry abut that."

"That's okay," Delaney said. "You want me to put my jacket back on? It doesn't really matter, though. I pretty much always look like a San Francisco longshoreman."

"No reason to put it on, then."

"Good. Let me get you a chair." He fetched a wooden chair from across the room and put it down in front of the desk, then walked around and seated himself on a chair with his jacket draped on the back.

Lancaster wasn't sure the wooden chair would hold him, but sat down anyway. It held, but he wondered for how long.

"What's your name, friend?" Delaney asked.

"Lancaster."

"You don't look local to me," the lawyer said. "Passing through?"

"I was," Lancaster said. "I've been here for about two days."

"And you already need a lawyer?"

"Well, I'm actually not here for me. It's for someone else. Somebody local."

"And who would that be?"

"Elizabeth Burkett."

"Burkett," Delaney said. "Wait, you mean . . . the judge's daughter-in-law?"

"That's right."

"What happened to her?"

"She was arrested."

"For what?"

"Killing her husband."

"Wait, wait," Delaney said, "I heard that Harry had been killed, but not that she did it. In fact, I heard there was a man who killed all the Burkett brothers."

Lancaster didn't say anything.

"Oh," Delaney said, staring at him.

"I didn't kill all the Burkett brothers," he said, "just three."

"And she killed Harry?"

"That's the way it looks right now."

"But not the way it is?" Delaney asked.

"Maybe not."

The lawyer sat back in his chair.

"How did all this happen?" he asked.

"I'll have to start at the beginning," Lancaster said, "but first I have a question to ask you."

"What's that?"

"Is this a case you'll want to take on if you have to go up against the judge?"

Delaney sat back in his chair.

"You don't just mean taking him on in court," Delaney said. "You mean taking on the judge personally."

"That's what I mean," Lancaster said, "but it could be damaging to your practice."

"Let me tell you something," Delaney said. "I don't have much of a practice to risk. And I wouldn't miss taking the judge on, believe me. I've always wanted to, but I've never had the right case. This? His daughter-in-law killing his son? This sounds a lot like the right case."

"What about your personal safety?" Lancaster asked. "What if that was at risk, as well?"

"Well . . . look at me. I'm a big guy and I can take care of myself. Also, from what I hear, you can handle a gun. I think I'll be fine."

"So you want to hear the story before you make your final decision?"

"I need to hear the story," Delaney said, "but not before I decide to take the case. I'm in."

"Okay, then," Lancaster said, "this is what happened. . . ."

Chapter Thirty-four

"Now, let me ask you a question," Delaney said, after Lancaster finished.

"What?"

"Do you believe Elizabeth when she says she doesn't remember shooting Harry?"

"I do," Lancaster said. "I was there and saw the look in her eyes. I thought she was in shock and the doctor confirmed it. I'm not only convinced she doesn't remember; I don't think she did it."

"What makes you so sure?"

"It's too pat that the other three brothers just happened to come along right after Harry was shot so they could find Liz with his body."

"You think somebody planned this?" Delaney asked. "And framed her?"

"That's what I think."

"Why would anybody do that?"

"That's the question," Lancaster said. "Look, what kind of shot do we have against the judge in court?"

"With a jury, we have some kind of shot," Delaney said. "Without a jury, we have none."

"But he wants his revenge to be legal, right?"

"Right."

"Then we need to find legal grounds to get Liz off," Lancaster said.

"With thinking like that," Delaney said, "what the hell do you need me for?"

"You're the legal brain, Mike," Lancaster said. "If I get you the evidence you need, can you present it to a jury so they'll find her not guilty?"

"You bet I can. But what about you?"

"I'm only in trouble if he convicts her," Lancaster said.

"You're right," Delaney said. "If she's convicted, she doesn't make a very creditable witness for you."

Delaney stood up and grabbed his jacket. "Let's get going," he said.

"Where?"

Delaney started putting on a tie.

"I've got to go see the judge and tell him I'm representing Elizabeth Burkett. Then I need to go to the jail and talk to her."

"Do I need to go with you?"

"That depends," Delaney said. "Do you want the judge to know you hired me?"

"Maybe I do," Lancaster said. "Maybe I can get under his skin that way."

"You're not going to get him to overreact," Delaney said. "He's just not known for losing control. I tell you what. I'll go see him alone, but when he asks who retained me, I'll tell him you did."

"Okay."

Delaney finished with his tie, adjusted his jacket, put on a black flat-brimmed Stetson, then turned and looked at Lancaster.

"How do I look?"

"Very legal."

"Good. The judge likes counsel to appear before him properly dressed. Now I'll go and talk to him and my client. You go and do what you have to do to figure out how to get Elizabeth back out to that house."

"You mean figure out how to break her out?"

"I didn't hear that."

They headed for the door.

"Wait," Lancaster said, "we didn't discuss your fee."

"If I can beat the judge on this case that'll be fee enough," Delaney said. "My practice will be set."

They came walking out of the alley and onto the main street when Lancaster asked, "What can you tell me about the sheriff?"

"You're not thinking about trusting him, are you?" the lawyer asked.

"I'm getting mixed signals from him," Lancaster said, "I was thinking about trusting him, but I've decided not to."

"Good," Delaney said. "Jessup will always have his own agenda. Don't trust anybody in this town, Lancaster. Not even me."

Chapter Thirty-five

Lancaster went to the livery to rent a horse.

"Only rentin' today?" the liveryman asked. "I thought we was talkin' about buyin'?"

"We were," Lancaster said. "Let me rent that six-year-old mare and by the time I get back I'll know if I want to buy her or not."

They agreed on a rental price. He tossed his saddle onto the mare and cinched it in. When he mounted up she felt good and solid underneath him.

He rode out to the Burkett place, dismounted and walked around the outside. Any tracks he might have found had been trampled by men from town coming to pick up the bodies. He walked behind the house, where there had been less foot traffic. There was no back door, but there were a few windows that would have made it accessible. He walked to each window, crouched down beneath each of them. Under the second window he found what he was looking for. A right boot print, one with a hole right where the ball of the foot would be. Now the sheriff was right about one thing. Lots of men had holes in the bottom of their boots. Plus, this track could have been made any time. But this was just too much of a coincidence to let it pass by.

Finished with his examination of the outside, he went inside the house. It had already been looted, since it had stood vacant with the door open for two days. Not that he'd noticed much that could be taken the first time he was there. He assumed anything that might have been of value was gone, but perhaps there were still things of sentimental value to Liz Burkett that might have still been there. He wouldn't know, of course, but that might be a way to lure her back out there.

He went into the bedroom, where the shooting had taken place. There was dried blood on the walls and the floor. He looked around but the shotgun had been taken. He tried to remember how the body had been lying, tried to reckon where the shooter would have been standing.

The major coincidence that bothered him was the victim's three brothers showing up at just the right time to catch Liz crouching over the body. Obviously she must have cradled the dead man in order to get that much blood on her. Why would she do that if she hated him? Perhaps in those moments before and after the shooting love and hate became intertwined. Maybe she wasn't cradling him; maybe she was just shaking him, beating on him for a change. In walked the brothers and, whether she shot him or not, they assumed she did. They dragged her outside to do what? Rape her?

Kill her? Both? He hadn't given the situation time to develop, so he couldn't tell.

He walked around the house, picking up something here and there, but there either wasn't much left to tell him about the people who lived there or the people who lived there didn't have much of a life. Usually when you were in a home you saw evidence of knitting or whittling or hunting, or something else to tell you the interests of the people who lived there.

There was nothing in this house at all.

He wondered idly whether the law or the looters had removed the murder weapon.

He decided to go back to town to find out.

As he entered the sheriff's office Jessup was coming out of the cellblocks with a tray.

"Did she eat?" he asked.

"Not much. Your lawyer was here."

"Her lawyer."

"Yeah, but you hired him, right?"

"Right."

Jessup shook his head.

"You should've asked me before you hired somebody. I could've given you some other names."

"What's wrong with Mike Delaney."

"Well," Jessup said, putting the tray down on his desk, "for one thing, the judge hates him."

"I thought the judge didn't feel love and hate."

"Well, maybe not love," Jessup said, "but he feels hate, all right, and he hates Delaney."

"Why?"

Jessup put both his hands up. "Ask Delaney. Look, I'm gonna take this tray back to the café and get somethin' to eat myself. Can you hang around here?"

"Sure. I wanted to talk to Liz anyway."

"Okay."

He picked up the tray, then put it down and stood there a moment, looking as though he was trying to make up his mind.

Lancaster walked over to a wall peg, took the cell key from it and handed it to the sheriff.

"Go ahead," he said, "take it with you. I don't want you to be worried the whole time you're out."

Jessup nodded, took the key and the tray and left the office.

Chapter Thirty-six

Lancaster walked into the cellblock and stopped in front of Liz's cell. She was sitting up with her hands clasped in her lap, her head down, staring at the floor. Her hair was hanging down, covering her face. He realized he'd never seen her hair clean, wasn't even sure what color it was. Could have been a dirty blonde, could have been brown.

"Liz?"

She looked up. Her face was cleaner than when he'd first seen her, of course. Maybe the doc or Rusty Connors had tried to clean her up. She had pale skin, some freckles on the bridge of her nose—she was pretty. And she looked young—very young.

"How old are you?"

"Twenty."

"How long were you married to Harry?"

"Two years."

"And how old was he?"

"Forty-one."

Twice her age.

"The sheriff says you talked with Mike Delaney."

"Yes," she said. "Thank you for sending him."

"I'm hoping he'll do us both some good," Lancaster said, "but that's only if we get to court."

"You don't think we will?"

"Well," Lancaster said, "I'm kind of hoping we won't. I'd rather not face the judge on his own turf."

"How do we avoid it?"

"By finding the truth before we get there."

"The truth?"

"Yes," he said. "Who killed Harry."

"Are you so convinced I didn't?" she asked.

"More and more."

"I don't know why," she said.

"Maybe because I've gotten to know you a little better as time has gone by. I just don't see you picking up a shotgun and blowing your husband's— sorry, killing your husband."

"Sometimes," she said, "I thought about killing him in his sleep, but I couldn't."

"And when he was beating you the other times? Did it ever occur to you?"

"No," she said. "The only thing I ever thought to do when he was beating me was to beg him to stop. That makes me kind of pathetic, doesn't it?"

"Not pathetic," Lancaster said. "But it also doesn't make you a killer."

She got up and walked toward the front of the cell. Hesitantly, she put her hands on the bars. "The lawyer was very nice," she said, "but I have to tell you something."

"The judge hates Mike."

"How did you know?"

"The sheriff told me."

"So you didn't know when you hired him?"

"No, I had no idea. Do you have any notion why the judge hates him?"

She turned and walked to the back of the cell, wringing her hands.

"This is something you'd find out anyway," she said, "so I have to tell you it has to do with . . . me."

"You? You mean . . . you and Mike Delaney?"

"We know each other," she said, "but I swear, nothing has ever happened between us."

"I think this is a story you better tell me, Liz. Now."

"All right," she said, sitting back down. Lancaster got a chair and sat down in front of the cell.

"When Harry and I came to town together he wanted to show me off, so we had a party. Lots of people from town came, including Mike. When we met we liked each other right away. I—I think he more than liked me."

"And you?"

"Yes," she said, "but there was nothing we could do about it. I was promised to Harry, and I went through with the wedding."

"And what happened?"

"I'd see Mike in town from time to time, and when . . . when Harry started beating me, Mike noticed the bruises. He and Harry got into a fight, and Mike beat him up."

"That's a reason for Harry to hate him," Lancaster said. "But learning what I have about the judge, I supposed he was embarrassed."

"Yes," she said, "and he's hated Mike ever since."

"Well," Lancaster said, "I'll talk to Mike and get his side of the story."

"Lancaster, I'll abide by any decision you make," she said. "If you think we should hire another lawyer, that's okay with me."

"Doc Meade," Lancaster said, shaking his head. "He knows all this, right?"

"Yes."

"And he and the judge don't like each other."

"No."

"So he sent me to Mike Delaney, knowing that if Delaney defended you in court it would get under the judge's skin. That old goat."

"Are you mad?" she asked. "At him? Or me?"

"I don't like being manipulated," Lancaster said. "But I'm not mad—not at you, anyway. It just seems like there are a lot of connections here I didn't know about."

"I guess they're becoming clear now," she said. She put her hands to her head. "If only my memory would become clear."

"Actually," Lancaster said, "that's what I came here to talk to you about."

"What?"

"There might be a way for us to jog your memory."

"How?"

"By taking you back to the house."

She hugged herself tightly.

"Oh, no," she said. "I can't go back there."

"Liz—"

"I can't," she said. "I can't go back into that house!"

"You want to remember what happened, don't you?" he asked.

"Yes."

"Well, I think this is the way."

"Lancaster—"

"Okay," he said, "think about it, will you? Just give it some thought. Okay?"

"Okay."

He heard the office door open, figured the sheriff was coming back.

"Liz, I went out to the house today to look around. It's a mess."

"I—I don't remember."

"Was there anything valuable there?" he asked. "I thought maybe someone had come in after we left and stolen some things."

"There was nothing to steal," she said. "Not really."

"Harry was the judge's son," Lancaster said. "Didn't he have any money? Any valuable possessions?"

"The judge has all that stuff," she said. "Not Harry, and not his brothers."

"The judge doesn't share, huh?"

"No," she said, "not with anybody."

"Okay," he said, "okay. I'll go have a talk with Mike and see you later."

When he came out of the cellblock he found the sheriff sitting at the desk, eating his supper.

"Thanks for stickin' around."

"I wanted to talk to her anyway."

"About what?"

"I think you know."

The sheriff looked at him.

"You know, when Mike Delaney walked in I thought, oh boy. Now it starts."

"Didn't think to tell me, huh?"

"That's up to her," Jessup said. "Not me. I figured you'd find out sooner or later what you were gettin' yourself into. Don't forget"—Jessup gestured with his knife— "I advised you to leave town."

"That's right, you did," Lancaster said. "All right if I come back later? I'm going to go and have some supper."

"Sure, come on back," Jessup said. "No skin off my nose if she has some visitors."

"Thanks, Sheriff," Lancaster said. "Oh, by the way, any luck hiring a deputy?"

"Nope. You interested?"

"No," Lancaster said, "I'm not really interested."

Chapter Thirty-seven

Lancaster invited Mike Delaney to have supper with him. Since it was Delaney's town, Lancaster let him choose the place. The lawyer took him to a small café he said he frequented because the price was cheap, but the food was good.

"I went to see Liz," Lancaster said.

"After me?"

"That's right."

"You want to hear how it went with the judge?" Delaney asked.

"After."

"After what?"

"After you tell me about you and Liz and Harry Burkett."

"You didn't know any of that when you came to see me?" the lawyer asked.

"No."

"Who told you?"

"Liz," Lancaster said. "Some of it. I want you to tell me all of it."

"Sure," Delaney said. "I'll tell you everything.

I love Liz—have since the first time I saw her. I wanted to marry her, but she had promised herself to Harry, so she went through with it."

"But that didn't sit well with you."

"Stuck in my craw," Delaney said. "Then, when she started showing up with bruises, I couldn't take it. I confronted Harry on the street."

"What did he say?"

"That it was none of my business," Delaney said. "He said a husband has the right to smack his wife around when she needs it. He said that's how his father and mother lived."

"What did you do?"

"I smacked him," Delaney said, "and then got into it. You can see I'm a big guy. It wasn't much of a fight. I left him lying in the street spitting out blood, dirt and teeth."

"And the judge didn't like it?"

"It embarrassed him to have his son whipped like that in front of the whole town."

"Take it out on you in court?"

"Naw," Delaney said. "I got to give it to the old man—he's usually pretty fair with me in court."

"So if he gets revenge on you, it will be legally?" Lancaster asked.

"I suppose."

"What about the brothers?" Lancaster asked. "Did they ever try to get revenge for Harry?"

"Sure," Delaney said. "All three of them jumped me outside my office one night."

"And?"

"I whipped them, too."

"They never came after you with guns?"

"All the Burkett boys were cowards, Lancaster," Delaney said. "The judge knew that. You know it. I heard what they were doing when you stopped them. Did they . . . did they . . ."

"Rape her? No. They knocked her around. I think they were getting ready to rape her . . . or kill her."

"Cowards."

"They drew on me."

"From what I heard, they didn't have a choice."

"They had a choice," Lancaster said. "I gave them plenty."

"Three-to-one odds," Delaney said, "and you were a stranger. They had no history to tell them they'd get beat."

The waiter came with their meals. Lancaster had let Delaney do the ordering. They got two steak platters with all the trimmings. They both dug in and concentrated on demolishing their meals.

"Say, that *was* pretty good," Lancaster admitted, when they were done.

"Told you."

"Thanks for picking this place."

"Thanks for paying," Delaney said. "I'm a little short these days."

After they ordered pie and coffee Lancaster said, "Okay, tell me what happened with the judge."

"Closest I ever saw him come to losing it was when I walked into his office and told him I was representing his daughter-in-law. But he kept his composure. He told me I'd better have a good case when I came into his court this time."

"Maybe this time he won't be so fair with you," Lancaster said.

"I guess we'll have to see," Delaney said. "You know, you don't strike me as the type of fella who solves his problems in court."

"I never have been," Lancaster said.

"And this time?"

"You get Liz off if she gets to court," Lancaster said. "I'll look after myself."

"You didn't get to Liz until after I did today," Delaney said. "Where else did you go?"

"Out to the house."

"What did you find?"

"Nothing," Lancaster said. "They didn't live well. When I walked in I thought the house had been looted, but Liz said there was nothing to steal."

"The judge doesn't share," Delaney said. "His boys had to make their own way in the world. Except for Harry. The judge got him his deputy's badge."

"Not much money in being a deputy," Lancaster said.

Delaney gave a crooked smile and said, "Not much in being a lawyer, either."

Lancaster paid the check and they left.

Out on the boardwalk in front of the café Lancaster asked, "Why not move to another town, start over with a new practice?"

149

"I'll do that," Delaney said, "when I get Liz off, and if she agrees to marry me and come with me."

"Tell me, do you think the judge has ever used a gunman to do his dirty work?"

"Not that I know of. Why?"

"There's a guy in town."

"A hired gun?"

"Yes."

"You think the judge brought him in for you?"

"I don't know," Lancaster said. "Maybe he was passing through and recognized me."

"Tell the sheriff."

"I'll handle it myself," Lancaster said. "If I have to."

Lancaster looked down at Delaney's boots.

"That your only pair of boots?"

Delaney looked down.

"Yeah, why? I can't really afford a new pair."

"Mind if I see the bottoms?"

"Why?"

"Humor me."

Delaney frowned.

"You're the one who told me not to trust anybody."

Delaney shrugged, lifted one boot, then the other. The bottoms were clean. No holes.

"Satisfied?"

"Yeah," Lancaster said, "I'm satisfied. Here." He took some money from his pocket and held it out.

"I told you I didn't want a fee for this."

"You may not want it, but you need it," Lancaster said. "Walking around money. Not enough for new boots, but enough for walking around."

Delaney smiled, said, "Everybody needs to walk around."

Chapter Thirty-eight

Lancaster woke the sheriff when he entered the office.

"Sorry."

Jessup dropped his feet off the desk and wiped his eyes.

"That's okay," he said. "Wanna talk to your girl again?"

"She's not my girl," Lancaster said, "but the answer is yes."

"Well, go ahead." He put his feet back on the desk and leaned back in his chair. "See if you can let yourself out without waking me again."

"Sure."

He walked into the cellblock, found Liz sitting the same way she was before, staring down.

"Liz."

She looked up. "Did you talk to Mike?"

"We talked."

"And?"

"He's hired."

She seemed relieved. "It's funny," she said. "I don't even know if he's a good lawyer."

"I guess that's something we'll have to find out together."

"Are you going to let him defend you in court?" she asked.

"Let's see what happens with you first. Have you thought about what I asked you?"

She hugged herself again. For a moment he thought she was going to lie down and curl up.

"I—I can't go back to the house."

"Liz," Lancaster said, "I don't think you killed Harry."

"What do you think happened?"

"I found some boot prints under one of your windows. I think somebody got in that way and killed Harry. I think they arranged to have his brothers show up so you'd get the blame."

"Somebody wanted those apes to kill me?"

"And then you'd get the blame for Harry."

"But . . . who would want to do that to me?"

"I think the question is, who wanted to kill Harry?" Lancaster said. "Or maybe killing Harry and framing you was someone's way of getting at the judge."

"The judge wouldn't care about me," she said, "and Harry always said the judge didn't care about anyone but himself."

"I'm learning that," Lancaster said. "I think I'm going to take a ride tomorrow and talk to the judge's wife."

"Mildred," Liz said. "She loved those boys, and she hated me. And the judge, well . . ."

"He used to beat her," Lancaster said.

"Maybe still does."

"Then maybe she'll have something to add to all this," he said.

"If the judge finds out you're going to talk to her . . ." she said in warning.

"I'll see if I can do it without him knowing," he said. "Then, after I've talked to her, I don't care if he finds out."

"Using Mike," she said, "and talking to Mildred—do you think you can push the Judge that way?"

"Maybe," Lancaster said. "Maybe we can get him to say or do something he doesn't want to do."

"He's a dangerous man."

"Even without his sons?"

"They were all kind of incompetent," she told him. "Mostly it's influence the judge uses. He has people convinced he's powerful and dangerous, so nobody ever challenges him."

"Well, then," Lancaster said, "that's what we have to do. Challenge him. If we can show the town he's not so powerful, maybe we can get them to turn on him."

"Then you won't have to worry about anyone taking a shot at you."

"We'll see about that," Lancaster said, thinking about Vincent Noble. "I'm going to go back to my hotel now. I'll see you in the morning."

She rushed to the front of the cell, took hold of the bars.

"Lancaster, do you really think I didn't kill Harry, after all?"

He put his hands over hers and said, "That's what I think, Liz."

"Oh, thank you," she said, pressing her forehead against one of his hands.

Now, he told himself, *the thing is going to be to prove it.*

Chapter Thirty-nine

It was too early to actually go back to his room, so Lancaster went to the Three Aces. Once again, as with the night before, action was in full swing. He stood just inside the batwing doors to survey the room, didn't see any of the three men who had been sitting with the drunken Hector Adams the night before. He walked to the bar, where he was able to elbow himself some room, and ordered a cold beer.

He was halfway through the first beer when the doors opened and Doc Meade came walking in. He was greeted by many of the men in the place jovially, enthusiastically. Obviously he was a well-liked man in Gallows.

He spotted Lancaster and came walking over to him.

"Looking for me, Doc?" Lancaster asked.

"Actually, no. I just had an urge for a cold beer, like the one you're holding."

"I'll get it for you."

Lancaster turned and signaled the bartender

for two more. When they came Lancaster handed the doctor his, set his now-empty first mug down on the bar and picked up his new one.

"Cheers," he said to the doc.

Meade raised his mug.

"How's Hector doing?" Lancaster asked.

"He'll be okay," the doctor said. "He's sober, so he's in more pain."

"Good," Lancaster said, "Maybe he'll learn not to be so stupid."

"That's what I told him."

"Oh," Lancaster said, "I found out why you sent me to Mike Delaney, you crafty old buzzard."

The doctor smiled and shook his head.

"Sorry," Meade said, "but I wanted you to find out the whole story."

"You could have just told me, you know."

"More fun this way."

"I'm glad somebody's having fun," Lancaster said. "Tell me, since you know so much, do you know a man named Vincent Noble?"

"Noble?" The doctor shook his head. "What's his part in all this?"

"I'm not sure," Lancaster said. "He wears black, except for a splash of maroon on his hat, his gun belt and a maroon vest. Have you seen him in town?"

"Nope, can't say I have."

Lancaster studied the old man.

"Sawbones, are you playing games with me? Because if you are, I'm going to get real sore."

"Well," Doc Meade said, "I *was* playin' games with ya, but now I've stopped. You know everythin'. Now I'm just gonna sit back and watch you take down the judge."

"What have you got against the judge?"

"I tell ya," Meade said. "it goes back so many years I don't think either one of us remembers what started it. It even goes back to before this town was called Gallows."

"Why *is* this town called Gallows?"

"For a while, the judge sort of fancied himself to be some kind of hangin' judge, only there was never anybody around to hang. But he decided to change the name of the town to Gallows anyway."

"What was it called before that?"

"Rosewood."

"Rosewood?" Lancaster asked. "You know, I've got to say I like Gallows better."

"I'll tell ya a secret," the doctor said. "So do I." He finished his beer, wiped off his mouth with the back of his sleeve. "I got to be goin'. Gotta check on Hector's wound. How is Elizabeth doin' in jail?"

"She's safe enough."

"Bet she's glad Mike will be defending her, huh?" the doctor asked.

"She's satisfied."

"And you?"

"I don't intend to get to court," Lancaster said. "I'm going to solve my trouble a different way."

"Do me a favor, then?"

"What?"

"Call the judge out into the street."

158

"Even if I did," Lancaster said, "do you really think he'd face me himself?"

"His boys are gone. Who do ya think . . . ? Oh, you mean this maroon gunman who's in town?"

"Maybe."

"Well, can't say it won't be interestin'. See you tomorrow, Lancaster."

"Night, Doc."

As the doctor left, Lancaster wondered whether he really did know everything now, or whether there were more surprises in store for him.

Chapter Forty

"Where's Stepmummy?" Vin asked.

"She's upstairs. She has a headache."

"Or a jaw ache?" Vin asked. "Maybe a stomach-ache? Where are you hitting her these days."

"I invited you here to have supper," the judge said. "Not to insult me."

"Was I insulting you?" Vin asked. "I thought I was making conversation."

"Have you seen Lancaster?"

Vin stared down the long table at his father as a woman dressed in white came out of the kitchen with some plates and set them on the table.

"Ah, family style?" Vin asked. "This is kind of a big table for that, but heck, I've got long arms. Yeah, I've seen him and talked to him."

He reached out and put some beef on his plate.

"Wait, you what? Talked to him? Did you tell him who you were?"

"Sure," Vin said. "In fact, we had breakfast together and introduced ourselves. Well, we didn't really have breakfast. He shared his second pot of coffee with me. This meat is really tender."

"Why did you do that?" the judge asked. "Did you tell him why you were in town?"

"You mean did I tell him I was here to kill him? No, I didn't say that. He sort of guessed, though."

"Vin, I don't know if that was wise."

"Why not?" Vin helped himself to some potatoes and onions. "Right now he's thinking about me, wondering what I'm really doing here, wondering when I'm going to try for him. He's not going to be able to relax."

"Well, maybe that's a good thing."

"You gonna haul this woman into court? Your daughter-in-law, I mean?"

"Yes," the judge said. "I'm going to put her on trial and make her pay for what she did to me."

"What she did to you? I thought it was poor Harry she killed,"

"She embarrassed me."

"Ah. You grow these onions yourself? They're really good."

"I think Cook has a garden out back."

"You think? Don't tell me you've never been in the kitchen or in the back of the house."

"What reason would there be for me to do either?" the judge asked, genuinely puzzled by the prospect.

"Never mind," Vin said. "You think Lancaster will be in court when the girl goes on trial?"

"Probably."

"You plan on putting him on trial, too?"

"Once she's convicted."

"And I'm supposed to kill him . . . when?"

161

"When I say so."

"So I'm just supposed to hang around and wait?"

"You're being paid."

"Yes, I am. You don't know what you want to do with him yet, do you? I've never known you to be . . . unsure before."

"I'm not unsure," the judge said. "I'm undecided. That's a totally different thing."

"I see." Vin reached out and snagged another piece of beef. "Mind if I get some more wine?"

"Help yourself."

Vin got up with his glass, walked to the sideboard and poured some red wine from a decanter. "You?"

"Please."

Vin walked to the table, filled his father's glass, then replaced the decanter before sitting back down.

"Where have you decided to stay?" the judge asked.

"I'm at the Dutchman," Vin said.

"Why there? To be close to Lancaster?"

"No," Vin said, "because it's the best hotel in town, and you're paying."

"You're playing a dangerous game, Vin."

"I know," Vin said. "I have to entertain myself while I'm waiting around for you to make up your mind."

"Lancaster is not a man to be trifled with," the judge said. "I checked him out."

"I know his background," Vin said, "but he's been out of the business for a while. He's rusty. That's too bad, actually."

"Why?"

"I'd like him to be at the top of his game when I kill him," Vin said.

"At the top of his game," the judge said, "he may kill you. Do you have help?"

"I have a couple of men coming to town," Vin said. "They'll be here tomorrow, but they're just backup. When the time comes, I'll do it myself. And speaking of that, you know the girl can suddenly show up dead in her cell."

"No," the judge said, "I'll be taking care of her legally."

"Hey," Vin said, "I'm just putting it out there."

"I'll keep it in mind."

Mildred Burkett sat on the bed in her bedroom, doubled over, holding her stomach. It was not because the judge had hit her. In fact, he had not. No, the pain she was feeling in her belly was due to the fact that Vin Noble—that creature—was in her house.

She hated Noble because he was the judge's firstborn, and because the judge had more feeling for him than he'd ever had for their four boys. As much feeling as the judge could have for anyone, of course.

The pain was real and palpable. She would know when Noble left her house—when the pain went away. But even then she wouldn't go downstairs. Not until the judge left to go to see his whore.

She had never been comfortable in this house. It had never been hers; it had always been only the judge's. Everything in it belonged to the judge.

Everything but her.

Chapter Forty-one

Lancaster had breakfast in the dining room of the Dutchman. Before going up to his room the night before he had checked with the desk clerk to see if Vincent Noble had checked into the hotel. He had. Lancaster asked the clerk who was paying for the room. As far as the man knew the guest was paying for his own room.

Then, just before he went up the stairs, Lancaster asked the clerk who owned the hotel.

"The judge."

Lancaster didn't see Vincent Noble at breakfast. He was pretty sure now that the judge had brought the man to town. The question was, exactly what for? And if it was to kill him, when? Would the judge try to get him legally first? And failing that, would he then unleash his killer? Or would the judge simply have Noble try to kill him before? He had the feeling the judge was going to concern himself first with his daughter-in-law.

After breakfast Lancaster walked to Mike Delaney's office, knocked and entered.

"Mornin'," Delaney said.

Lancaster nodded, seated himself.

"I'm convinced the judge has brought a killer named Vincent Noble to town."

"To kill you?"

"That's what I figure."

"When?"

"That I don't know," Lancaster said. "I talked with the man at breakfast yesterday morning, but he wasn't giving anything away."

Delaney leaned back in his chair. "I think the judge will go after you legally first, Lancaster," he said, "before he uses a hired killer against you."

"That's what I was thinking, but there's no way to be sure."

"So you'll have to watch your back."

Lancaster smiled. "Something I've never fallen out of the habit of doing."

"I'm supposed to check with the judge today to see if he's set a court date for Liz."

"How soon do you think he'll schedule it?" Lancaster asked.

"A day or two, at the most."

"Okay. I've got some things to do, so I'll see you later and find out." He stood up.

"Whoa, what kind of things? Anything I should know about?"

At the door Lancaster turned and replied, "I'm going to take a ride out to the judge's house and talk to his wife."

"You think that's wise?"

"He won't be there, will he?"

"No," Delaney said. "He's always in his office in the morning."

"Well, then, why not?" Lancaster asked. "Let's see what the lady has to say about her husband. And about the death of her sons."

"You think she'll talk to the man who killed three of them?"

"I don't know," Lancaster said. "I'm just going to ride out there and find out."

"Well, good luck," Delaney said. "Let's hope the lady doesn't save a lot of people a lot of trouble and kill you herself."

"I'll be on my guard."

Chapter Forty-two

As it turned out Lancaster did not have to ride to the home of the judge and his wife. All he needed to do was walk. The judge lived in a large house that stood alone just outside of town, just to the north. It had white columns, looked as if it had been fashioned after some of the big Southern plantation homes.

He approached the house, found it to be in perfect repair. He wondered whether that was due to the judge or his wife.

He was hit with second thoughts as he walked to the door. This woman was not going to be too thrilled to meet the man who had killed three of her sons. Then again, maybe she'd be so upset that she'd say something about the judge that he could use.

He used the large metal knocker, which was in the shape of a horse's head, to knock on the door. The door was opened by a black man wearing a white jacket and white gloves.

"Yes, suh?"

"I'd like to see Mrs. Burkett, please."

"Who shall I say is callin', suh?" The man had white peppered in his black hair, and the black skin of his face had a chalky look. These were the only indications that he might be as old as sixty. He stood straight and tall and stared Lancaster right in the eyes.

"My name is Lancaster."

A look of horror came over the man's face. He stepped outside, actually pushed Lancaster back a few steps so he could close the door behind him.

"Suh, it would not be a good thing for Mrs. Burkett to see you."

"You know who I am?"

"Yes, suh, you killed those no-account sons of hers. No loss to the world, suh, I can tell you, but the missus is very upset about it. If you was to talk to her, I don't know what she'd do."

"I see. What's your name?"

"Ronald, suh."

"Ronald, do you work for Mrs. Burkett, or do you work for the judge."

"I works for the judge, suh, for many years."

"So you're loyal to him?"

"I hates him, suh."

"Then why work for him?"

"I don't got no place else ta go."

"And how do you feel about Mrs. Burkett?"

"I feels sorry for her."

"Why?"

"Because she's in the same position as me, suh,"

Ronald said. "She hates the judge, but got no-
where else ta go."

"Ronald, the judge is going to try to put me away
for killing his three sons."

"No, suh," Ronald said, "he gonna try ta put
you away for embarassin' him."

"Does everybody know this about the judge?"
Lancaster asked.

"Oh, yes, suh."

"Why are you talking to me like this, Ronald?
If the judge found out he'd fire you."

"If'n the judge found out, he'd kill me, suh."

"Then why?"

Ronald shrugged. "I done lived long enough,
suh."

"You really don't think Mrs. Burkett would talk
to me?"

"No, suh."

"How about if you tell her I'm out to get the
judge before he gets me."

"I reckon that'd give her a hard decision to
make," Ronald said, rubbing his jaw.

"How's that?"

"Well, suh, you the man who killed her boys,
but if'n you was truly goin' to take down the
judge, I think she might like ta help ya."

"Ronald, why don't you go ask her," Lancaster
said, "and I'll abide by whatever decision she
makes."

"Well, suh, I guess I could ask. Wait here,
please."

* * *

Back In town the three friends, Jelly Simms, Winston Hunter and Zack Teller, were in the Three Aces saloon, talking to a bunch of other men who had known the Burkett brothers.

"Them other three, they were no-account—we all know that," Simms said.

"Hell," another man said, "we're all no-account, Jelly."

The men laughed.

"That's right," Simms said, "but Harry, he was a deputy, and that woman killed him. I say she ain't gonna get away with it."

"I say we go over to that jail, take 'er out and hang 'er," Teller said.

"Hang a woman?" someone said.

"Hang a murderer," Hunter said. "What's the difference if it's a man or a woman? We can't let a murderer get away with it."

"But . . . the judge'll take care of her in court," someone else said.

"We got to do this for the judge," Simms said. "After everythin' he's done for this town, we gotta do this so he don't hafta go to court against his own daughter-in-law. We owe that to him!"

Again a cheer went up from the men, and somebody called for a rope.

The bartender, looking worried, slipped out the back and went over to the sheriff's office.

Lancaster waited a good fifteen minutes. The woman must have been giving the matter a lot of thought. Could she be in the same room with the man who killed three of her sons? Was her hatred of her husband strong enough to offset the balance?

Then the front door opened and Ronald said, "Won't you come in, suh?"

Chapter Forty-three

"I hope you don't mind talking in the kitchen, Mr. Lancaster," Mildred Burkett said. "It's the only room in the house my husband has never been in. Consequently, it's the only room in the house that is truly mine—mine and Cook's." She inclined her head toward a woman in white who was standing at the stove.

"I don't mind, ma'am," Lancaster said. "I'm just glad you agreed to talk to me."

Mildred Burkett, wearing a powder blue robe, was sitting at the kitchen table. She was in her sixties, but Lancaster thought she looked older. Probably because she had come down directly from her bedroom and had not even combed her hair.

"You killed my sons, Mr. Lancaster," she said. "What could you possibly want from me?"

"Your sons gave me no choice, ma'am," Lancaster said. "They were going to kill your daughter-in-law, and when I stopped them, they drew on me."

"And you are a professional gunman," she said. "My boys had no chance against you."

"They should've known that, ma'am," he said. "Somebody should've taught them better."

"Like who? Their father? Their father couldn't care less about them. If he did care, you'd be in jail."

"I was in jail, ma'am. Now your daughter-in-law is in jail."

"Both of you should rot there."

"Ma'am, your son used to beat your daughter-in-law, Liz," Lancaster said. "If you'll excuse me, she said he learned that from his father."

"Really? So he learned something from his father, eh?" she said.

The cook, a heavyset woman in her fifties, put a cup of coffee in front of her mistress.

"Coffee for Mr. Lancaster, Cook," Mildred said. "Coffee for the man who killed my boys."

"No, thanks," Lancaster said. "That's fine."

"Mr. Lancaster," Mildred said, "the only reason I agreed to see you is that Ronald told me that you're after my husband."

"As I see it," Lancaster said, "I have to get him before he gets me."

"You're a gunman," she said. "Why don't you just do us all a favor and kill him."

"I can't just kill him, ma'am," Lancaster said. "That would be murder."

"And he wants to put you away legally," she said. "You're both so legal."

"Ma'am," he said, "I need a way to get to your husband. Do you know of one?"

"The only thing he values is his reputation," she

said. "And the only thing you can hurt on him is his ego."

"All right," he said, figuring he'd gotten all he could get out of her. "Thank you, Mrs. Burkett, and for what it's worth . . . I'm sorry."

He turned to leave until Mildred said, "There's something you should know, Mr. Lancaster."

"What's that, ma'am?"

"My husband is a big man in this town, and in this county, but the county line ends about five miles outside of town, to the south. Ride that way and you'll be in Eddy County."

He nodded, waited for more.

"Go and talk to some people in the next county," she said. "Talk to some people in the towns of Tateville or Garner. Talk to them."

"Okay," he said, when nothing else was forthcoming. "Thank you, Mrs. Burkett."

As he walked to the front door, led by Ronald, she began to scream from the kitchen.

"And if you ever come back here again, I'll kill you myself!"

Ronald stepped outside with Lancaster and closed the door.

"What did she mean about those other towns?" he asked the black man.

"Her sons used to go there," she said. "The judge didn't care how they acted when they were outside his county."

"I see," Lancaster said, "so I'll find out some things about the sons that maybe people here don't know."

"And maybe some things about the judge."

"Like what—?" Lancaster started to ask, but Ronald had stepped back inside and closed the door.

Chapter Forty-four

It was getting dark when Lancaster got back to Gallows, so the lit torches in front of the jail were very obvious. There were quite a few of them and, as he got closer, he saw that there was a crowd of men there, as well.

He tied up his horse down the street, then pushed through the crowd to get to the office door and went inside. He pulled up short when he found himself looking down the barrel of a shotgun held by Sheriff Jessup.

"Oh," Jessup said, lowering the gun, "I thought one of those morons had got brave on me."

"Are they here for what I think they're here for?" Lancaster asked.

"Yeah, somebody got 'em all riled up about Liz killing Harry and somebody out there's got a rope."

"They haven't tried to come in yet?"

"No."

"How long have they been out there?"

"About an hour."

"I notice they're passing around bottles of whiskey, so they're going to get brave soon."

"You gonna stand 'em off with me?"

"Would you do it without me?"

"It's my job."

"Well, don't worry," Lancaster said, "if they want her they'll have to go through both of us."

"Grab a shotgun from the rack."

Lancaster walked over to the gun rack, took down a twelve-gauge side-by-side Colt shotgun and started to load it.

"You'll need one of these, too."

He turned as Jessup dropped a deputy's star on the desk. It landed with a tinny ring.

"What for?"

"If for no other reason," the sheriff said, "it gives them somethin' to shoot at."

Lancaster thought Jessup wanted him to wear a badge just to get under the judge's skin. He didn't think it was such a bad idea.

"Okay," Lancaster said, pinning it on. "You wanna go out there and call their bluff?"

"You think they're bluffin'?"

"I think," Lancaster said, "if we get them while they're still reasonably sober we can convince them they're bluffing. The thing about a mob is, nobody wants to be the first one killed."

Lancaster walked into the cellblock. Liz was standing at the front of her cell, gripping the bars.

"What's happening?" she asked. "It sounds like . . . like a crowd outside."

"Not a crowd," he said. "A mob."

"A lynch mob?" she asked, panicky.

"Don't worry," Lancaster said. "They're not going to get in."

"How are the two of you going to stop them?" she asked.

"By killing them, if we have to."

"Killing them?" she asked. "You mean . . . all of them?"

"All of them."

"For me?"

"For both of us, Liz." He put a hand over one of hers. "Don't worry."

"Don't worry?" she asked. "Once you get out that door, I don't know who's going to come back in."

"That's okay," Lancaster said. "I do."

Chapter Forty-five

Simms, Hunter and Teller were standing apart, in different parts of the crowd. Theirs were the voices, however, that kept egging on the crowd. Also, they were the three who had brought whiskey bottles with them and started passing them around.

Hunter and Teller kept doing what Simms had told them to do. Every time the crowd's enthusiasm for a hanging seemed to flag, they would begin stoking the fires again. Even Eddie Pratt, whose best friend was the ex-deputy, Hector Adams, was involved. He was the drunkest member of the crowd, and he was front and center, holding a torch and shouting obscenities.

When the door to the jail finally opened Sheriff Jessup stepped out with Lancaster behind him—and Lancaster was wearing a deputy's badge.

Lancaster stepped outside right behind Sheriff Jessup, looked over the mob. He was hoping to find a face he knew, didn't see any in front, so he started searching throughout the mob. Finally, he saw one of the three men who had convinced Hector Adams to go after him. If he was here, so were the other two. He still didn't know their names, but this was the time to find out.

The crowd fell quiet as the sheriff raised his hand.

"Time for you to go home, people. You're not gonna get your way here tonight."

"You're outnumbered, Sheriff," Eddie Pratt shouted from the front of the mob.

"And you're drunk, and we're sober," Jessup said. "You leadin' this pack, Pratt?"

"What's he doin' wearin' Hector's badge?" Pratt demanded.

"Or is that Harry's badge?" someone shouted.

"It's my badge," Jessup said. "Mine to give to whoever I want."

"Sheriff, you can't—"

"Pratt's not leading this mob, Sheriff," Lancaster said aloud.

"What?" Jessup said.

"There's a man back there. See him? Tall, skinny, kinda homely. Him and two of his friends. Wait, there's another one."

"Is that . . . Winston Hunter?" Jessup said. "And that's Jelly Simms."

"And look where they are," Lancaster said, loudly. "In the back, where's it's safe to start trouble and hide. Do they have a friend?"

181

"Yeah," Jessup said, "his name's Teller. Where's Zack Teller?"

The crowd started to get loud again, led by Pratt, so Jessup pointed his shotgun at the sky and let one barrel go. Everybody got quiet. Lancaster counted twenty-five, maybe thirty men.

"Zack Teller!" Jessup said.

The crowd parted, leaving Teller standing alone.

"Simms and Hunter, get over there by Teller—now!" Jessup said.

Slowly Simms and Hunter joined their partner.

"Okay," Lancaster said, "now, I'm going to bet that it was these three who started talking about a lynch mob. Am I right?"

A couple of men said, "Yeah" and "Right."

"And I'm gonna bet they brought whiskey to the party and started passing it around. Am I right?"

This time four or five men said, "Yes."

"Then you fellas don't really want to be here," Jessup said.

"And you don't want to hang anybody," Lancaster said. "These three have been getting you liquored up and egging you on."

The men started looking around at one another, but one who didn't seem to believe a word was Eddie Pratt.

"Don't listen to them," Pratt said. "Look, we're all friends of Hector Adams and Harry Burkett, and now one's dead and the other one has been

shot and had his badge taken away—by this man!"
He pointed at Lancaster. "I say we go over these
two and hang the woman."

"Okay, Pratt," Lancaster said. "Let's say you're
the leader of this mob. Then you come ahead. Be
first. Take a bullet so that the rest of this mob can
roll over us and hang the girl."

"Don't listen to him," Pratt shouted. "Go on!
Take them."

"There, see?" Lancaster shouted. "He wants
you to be first. So come on, who's it going to be?"

"Who's first?" Jessup asked, leveling his shotgun at the crowd. "Who's the first to get a face
full of buckshot?"

Lancaster pointed his shotgun at the crowd
and waited.

Nobody moved.

Except Pratt. He turned and walked back to
where Simms, Hunter and Teller were standing.

"Let's take 'em," he said. "The four of us. We can
do it."

"We'll take 'em," Simms said. "But not now.
Not while they're ready."

"So what was all this for?" Pratt asked.

"It was just a shot," Simms said, "tryin' to see if
we could get a mob to take 'er out and hang 'er,
maybe take care of the two of them at the same
time."

"I say we do it . . . now!" Pratt said, going for
his gun and turning.

"No!" Simms said.

The crowd parted as Pratt brought his gun up. Hunter and Teller, feeling they were in the line of fire and had no choice, also drew. Simms dropped to the ground.

Lancaster never hesitated. He pulled both triggers and sent two loads of twelve-gauge buckshot flying toward the three men. As their guns went off the sheriff pulled the remaining trigger on his gun.

Each of the three men got one shot off before their bodies were riddled with shot and dumped on the ground. The crowd scattered, leaving only the three dead men and Jelly Simms, staring at his friends' dead bodies.

Jessup and Lancaster stepped into the street. Lancaster drew his pistol just in case. They checked the three men to be sure they were dead, and then Jessup yanked Simms to his feet.

"This what you wanted?" he asked. "Dead friends?"

"I—I didn't—"

"Time for you leave town, Simms," Jessup said.

"Wha—Hey, I live here!"

"No anymore," Lancaster said. "Starting tomorrow morning, if I see you, I'll kill you."

A few stragglers were nearby, and Jessup called them over to remove the bodies.

Across the street, hidden by the darkness of a doorway, Vin Noble watched the entire proceedings. He was impressed with Lancaster's calm in the face of the mob. He never hesitated to pull the trigger. But that had been with the shotgun. He still hadn't seen his moves with his sidearm. He stepped out of the doorway and walked off.

Chapter Forty-six

"He did what?" the judge asked incredulously.

"Your lawman stuck a badge on Lancaster."

"That's preposterous."

"Well," Vin said, "he needed someone to help him hold back the lynch mob."

"What lynch mob."

"The one that tried to string up your daughter-in-law tonight," Vin said. "Or should I say my half sister-in-law?"

Vin had found the judge right where he thought he would, still in his office even at this late time.

"What the hell happened?" the judge asked. "Did they hang her?"

"No. Jessup and Lancaster stood them off. Had to kill three of them to do it. Lancaster was good. No hesitation at all."

"You sound impressed."

"I was."

"Is he too good for you?"

"Not from what I saw tonight," Vin said.

"And did your two men arrive in town today?"

"They did," Vin said. "Came in without too

186

many people seeing them. They'll be around if I need them."

"Well, I've got to head home."

"Home?"

The judge stood up. "Never mind," he said, "it doesn't matter where I'm going. You better just stay out of trouble until I need you."

"Yes, Daddy."

"Why must you taunt me all the time?"

Vin shrugged. "It just seems to come naturally."

Jessup and Lancaster went back into the sheriff's office, replaced the shotguns in the gun rack after reloading them. Then Lancaster went in to see Liz

"Oh, thank God," she said, going limp with relief. "I heard the shots."

"We had to kill three," he said.

"Three . . ." Liz shook her head. "And Harry, and his brothers . . . So many dead . . ."

"And they all made their own choices," Lancaster pointed out.

"I suppose so." She went back to her bunk and sat down.

"Liz, I spoke to your mother-in-law today."

"She hated me, too."

"Sounds like she hated everyone but her boys."

"Well, she was their mother. I don't suppose she saw all their faults."

"Or she saw them and loved them anyway."

Liz suddenly hugged herself tightly around the stomach.

"Are you all right? Do you feel sick?"

"No," she said, "I was just thinking . . . I can't believe I was ever considering having a baby with Harry."

"You can still have babies, Liz," Lancaster said. "You're young."

"How will I ever find the right man?" she asked. "They all seem so . . ." She didn't finish her sentence.

"Let's concentrate on getting you free first," Lancaster said, "then you can worry about finding the right man."

"Do you really think there are any out there?" she asked.

"I'm sure of it," Lancaster said. "Are you hungry?"

"I could use . . . something."

"I'll talk to the sheriff."

He went out into the office, found Jessup sitting at his desk. Lancaster took off the deputy's badge and laid it on the desk.

"What're ya doin'?" Jessup asked.

"I don't need it anymore," he said.

"Why not?"

"The emergency is over," Lancaster said, "and I have to leave town for a while tomorrow."

"To go where?"

"To find out some things about the judge and his boys."

"I don't know what you think you're gonna find," Jessup said, "but nobody in this county is gonna talk against the judge."

"That's what I'm counting on."

Jessup frowned.

"I don't get it," he said.

Lancaster was impressed that Jessup had gone out to face the lynch mob to keep Liz safe. He felt sure the sheriff would have done it alone if he had to. But he didn't trust the man enough to tell him what all his plans were for the next day.

"That's okay," Lancaster said. "Don't worry about it."

"Did you go and talk to the judge's wife?"

"I did."

"What did she have to say?"

"She said if I ever came back there," Lancaster answered, "she'd kill me herself." He walked to the door. "I should be back by the end of the day tomorrow."

"And if you don't come back at all?" the sheriff asked.

"Well, then, you better figure that I'm dead," Lancaster said, "because that's the only way I won't come back."

Instead of going back to his hotel after talking with the Judge, Vin walked over and took up a position across from the jail. He just wanted to see what went on there in the evening. He saw Lancaster leave and walk in the direction of the Dutchman Hotel. He noticed that he was no longer wearing the deputy's badge. Guess he only needed it to stand off that mob.

He considered going into the jail just to talk to

189

the sheriff for a while, maybe introduce himself, but that probably wasn't a smart thing to do. Better to keep the law in the dark about him—although he wondered whether Lancaster had told the lawman about him already.

No, he had a better idea. He'd go to see the two men he had brought to town to back his play. Make sure they knew what they were all going to be up against.

Lancaster may not be the man he once was with a gun, but he didn't seem to have lost his nerve.

Chapter Forty-seven

The next morning Lancaster rode out of Gallows and headed south. Soon he was out of Chavez County and in Eddy.

First he went to Tateville, stopped into the sheriff's office.

"Lancaster," the sheriff said. "I know that name."

"From a long time ago, Sheriff," Lancaster said. "There are no wants out on me."

"I know that," the lawman said. "My name is Ingles—been the law here for almost twelve years."

"That's a long time to wear a badge in one place."

"I know. I like it here. Almost fifty now—don't want to have to go and find a job somewhere else."

"Can't blame you for that."

"What can I do for you, Lancaster?" Ingles asked. "Have a seat."

"I assume you know who Judge Burkett is," Lancaster said, sitting down.

"Sure, everybody knows the judge from Chavez County."

"What do you know about him?"

"I know he's got four no-account sons who used to come here and abuse people. But . . . .I heard they were all dead?"

"That's right."

"You killed them?"

"Three of them," Lancaster said. "Let me tell you what happened, and what I need. Okay?"

Ingles put his feet up on the desk and said, "I'm all ears."

"So I'm thinking I've got to find something to take back to Gallows that will show people who the judge really is. Who his sons were. And to wake them up to the fact that it's time to stand up to him."

"I don't think that's gonna be easy," Sheriff Ingles said. "Chavez County has been under the judge's thumb for a lot of years."

"Well, I at least need something that will prove Liz Burkett had no choice but to kill her husband."

"I know plenty of husbands who knock their wives around, Lancaster," Ingles said.

"And you think that's okay?"

Ingles shrugged. "I guess that depends on what she did to deserve the smack."

"And do you smack your wife?"

"Are you kiddin'? If I did, she'd kill me in my sleep."

"Well, maybe Liz Burkett waited and did it while her husband was awake."

"Okay, look, go over to Maisie's and talk to some of the girls."

"Cathouse?"

"The best in town," Ingles said. "That's where the Burkett boys go—or went—when they came to town. You might find out something useful there."

"Thanks, Sheriff," Lancaster said. "Anybody in particular I should ask for?"

"No—well, yeah, the owner. Her name is Maisie." He saw the look on Lancaster's face. "It's not just a name, you know?"

"How do I find it?"

"Come on," the sheriff said, "I'll show you. . . ."

The sheriff had taken him to the door and pointed out Maisie's, which was about a block away. Lancaster walked over and knocked on the door. It was opened by a small girl in a white robe. She had an exquisite face and beautiful body, but she probably was not even five feet tall.

"Yes?"

"I'm looking for Maisie."

"It's early," the girl said. "We're not really open for business yet."

"That's okay," Lancaster said. "I just want to ask her some questions, and maybe talk to some of the girls."

"I'll ask her," the girl said. "What is it about?"

"It's about Judge Burkett's sons."

The girl's eyes widened. "Wait here," she said.

"I'll ask Maisie if she'll talk to you. What's your name?"

"My name is Lancaster," he said. "I just rode over from Gallows."

"Lancaster?"

"That's right."

She nodded, backed into the house and closed the door behind her.

Chapter Forty-eight

Moments later the door was opened by a woman in her forties who had once been a great beauty. But that had been some years and many pounds ago. Now she pulled a thin wrap around her over-ripe body and stared at Lancaster.

"You're the man who killed three of the Burkett boys?" she asked.

"That's right."

Suddenly she smiled.

"Well, you come right on in, Mister," she said. "Any of my girls you want, it's on the house."

She grabbed his hand and pulled him inside. He found himself in an entry foyer with a curtained doorway to his right and a stairway right across from him.

"So, you want a girl?" she asked.

"I want as many girls as you have," he said, "who can tell me something about the Burkett boys."

"All of them?"

"All the Burketts? Yes, if Harry was also a customer of yours."

"Oh, Harry was a customer, all right," she said.

"Him and his brothers have left more girls bruised than any other twenty men I've had here."

"I'd like to talk to any of the girls they hurt."

"Why?"

"Well, Harry's wife is going to go on trial for killing him," he said. "I want to prove that all the Burkett men were violent toward women, and that she was acting in self-defense when she shot him."

"Not a chance."

"Not a chance . . . I can talk to the girls? Or not a chance of proving—"

"All of it," she said.

"Why?"

"Well, first, she's gonna be appearing in front of the judge, right?"

"That's right."

"And he's gonna pick the jury?"

"I guess."

"You ain't ever gonna get a jury to acquit that woman for killing the judge's son."

"But she had no choice," he said.

"I don't doubt it. All those men deserved to be killed, including the judge."

"Was he ever a customer here?"

"For years, until he got married and acquired a mistress," Maisie said. "I guess he took all his violent tendencies out on them instead of my girls. Sorry the same can't be said for his sons. But thanks to you, they won't be coming around here anymore. You sure you don't want a free poke?"

"I need help, Maisie," Lancaster said, "not a free poke."

"Look," she said, "the Burketts may be dead, but the judge is alive. None of my girls is going to go into his court and go against him.'

"What about Garner? Is there a whorehouse there?"

"Yes," she said, "and they also are grateful that the Burketts are dead, but they won't send their girls into court, either."

"I need to show the whole town of Gallows that the Burketts brutalized women," Lancaster said. "Maybe I can do that with one girl?"

Maisie crossed her arms in front of her ample bosom. "No," she said.

"How about if I ask them."

"No."

"How about if you ask them?"

She chewed her lip, then said, "Wait here."

She went through the curtained doorway he assumed led to a sitting room with her girls in it. He heard her voice drone on, waited, didn't hear any other voices in reply. Then she came back.

"Sorry," she said. "My girls won't go against the judge."

"Look," he said, trying one last time, "this could finish the judge. I might be able to get the government to pull him off the bench."

"You're dreamin', Mr. Lancaster," she said. "If you want to get the judge off the bench, you're gonna have to kill him."

"Okay," he said, shaking his head, "I'll just ride over to Garner and ask—"

"The Garner house and I rotate girls in and

out," she said. "We're partners. You're just gonna waste your time if you ride over there. You're gonna get the same answer."

Lancaster stared at her, but she held his stare and never wavered.

"Now, how about that free one?" she asked. "Angie, the girl who let you in? She kinda likes you."

"No, thanks," he said. "Do you know of any other women in town who might have had trouble with the Burketts?"

"You mean decent women? A decent woman wouldn't spit on those boys."

Lancaster felt helpless. "I don't have another way to go," he said.

"You have a gun," she said. "Isn't that the way you usually solve your problems?"

"Ma'am," he said, "this gun is what got me into this mess."

Chapter Forty-nine

A decent woman wouldn't spit on the Burketts, Maisie had told him. And the whores wouldn't speak out against them, not in the judge's court.

As he rode back into Gallows later that afternoon he wondered whether he could get another judge to help him with a change of venue. But he doubted the judge would let go of this. And he doubted any other judge would act against him. Somebody in the government could have, but Lancaster didn't have those kinds of connections. He'd been a hired gun most of his life, and a drifter these past few years. You don't make friends in high places with those kinds of credentials.

He reined in his horse in front of the jail and dismounted. But he stopped short of going inside. Instead he walked the horse to Mike Delaney's office, tied it off in front of the hardware store. He went up the stairs and knocked on the door.

"Come on in!"

He opened the door and went in.

"Lancaster," Delaney said, "I've been lookin' for you. We have a court date."

"When is it?"

"Day after tomorrow."

"He can get a jury together that fast?"

"Haven't you figured out by now the judge can do practically anything he wants?"

"If she goes to court, she's going to lose, Mike. He'll sentence her to death."

"Thanks for the vote of confidence."

"You know it, too, don't you?"

"Yeah, I know it." Delaney sat back in his chair. "I don't know what else to do but go through the motions."

"I went to Tateville today to talk to some of the . . . women there, to see if they wanted to help."

"You went to Maisie's?"

"Yeah."

"And?"

"Maisie wouldn't even let me talk to the girls about testifying."

"About what?"

"About the Burkett boys beating them up."

"Ah, you want to show the jury how brutal they were."

"Yeah."

"So they'll realize that Liz was justified in shooting her husband."

"Yes," Lancaster said, "if she shot him." He told Delaney about finding the same footprint outside one of Liz's windows that he had found outside the window of his cell.

"Lots of men have holes in their boots, Lancaster," Mike said. "That's why you wanted to look at mine, right?"

"Right."

"Well," Delaney said, "we could go around town looking at everybody's boots."

"Yeah, we could."

"What other option do we have?"

"Maisie pointed one out to me."

"What's that?"

"She said I should use my gun."

"Kill the judge?"

Lancaster nodded.

"You considering it?"

Lancaster didn't answer.

"I thought those days were over for you," Delaney said.

"So did I," Lancaster said, "but my gun got me into this. Maybe it should get me—and Liz—out."

"Well, if you're right about there being a gunman in town gunning for you, you might be right. Maybe you could get to him first, make him tell you who hired him?"

"Yeah, maybe," Lancaster said.

"I can maybe use this stuff about the boot prints in court," Delaney said. "It's not real evidence, but maybe the jury will buy it."

"If the jury finds her innocent," Lancaster asked, "can the judge overturn the verdict? I mean, legally?"

"Sure," Delaney said. "It's his court. He plays God even more in there than he does outside."

"Can't he be reported? I mean, to somebody . . . higher up?"

"The higher-ups in the state capital think the world of the judge," Delaney said. "They don't know about any of this stuff."

"Maybe somebody should tell them."

"Yeah," Delaney said, "somebody with connections."

"You know somebody like that?" Lancaster asked. "I mean, somebody with connections?"

"Sure," Delaney said.

"Who?"

"The judge."

"Great suggestion."

"Or," Delaney added with a grin, "you could try the doc."

Chapter Fifty

Lancaster entered the doctor's office and yelled, "Hey, Doc."

"In here," the doctor yelled from his examination room. "I'm with a patient. Be right out."

Lancaster stood at the window looking out while he waited. Eventually the doctor came out with a woman and a little girl. The girl had a bandage on her knee and was limping more than was necessary.

"Do I got to stay home from school tomorrow, Doc?" she asked. "It hurts an awful lot."

The mother smiled at the doctor, then dropped the smile when she saw Lancaster.

"The best thing for it, Milly, is to walk on it," the doctor told the child. "You got to go to school."

"Aw, Doc . . ."

"Thanks, Doc," Milly's mother said, and rushed the child out the door.

"Don't mind Mrs. Benson," the doctor said. "By now most folks in town know what you did, and they know you're tryin' to help Liz."

"And they don't approve?"

"They're scared," he said.

"Of what?"

"Change," the doctor said. "If you beat the judge, things will change. They're just not sure it will be for the better."

"And how do you feel about change?"

"Heck, I embrace it," the doctor said. "We're less than fifteen years from a new century. That's gonna be some change. I hope I'm around to see it."

"How old would you be then?"

"Eighty, thereabouts."

"You'll make it."

"I think so, too," Doc Meade said. "And I hope you will, too."

"You don't think I will if I keep going up against the judge?"

The doctor shrugged.

"Doc, I think somebody should let the folks at the state capital know what's going on here."

"You?"

"I don't know anybody there," Lancaster said. "But someone told me you do."

"Is that a fact? And you want me to go to them and complain about the judge?"

"Why not?"

"Like I told you," Meade said, "I wanna see that new century."

"The judge would kill you?" Lancaster asked. "Or have you killed?"

"I wouldn't want to test him."

"Well, maybe I should take Maisie's advice," Lancaster said.

"What did that old whore tell you to do?"

"Go back to the way I was," Lancaster said. "Use my gun to solve the problem."

"Kill the judge? In cold blood?"

"It would solve a lot of people's problems."

"Yeah, and give you a whole new set. You'd be on the run for sure."

"Liz would be safe," Lancaster said, "And so would this town."

"You haven't been here long enough to make that judgment," the older man said. "How do you know this town, this county, would be better off without the judge?"

"It would be hard for it not to be," Lancaster said. "What about the judge's wife?"

"What about her?"

"You probably treated her for bruises, broken bones, like you did Liz?"

"I treat lots of women for bumps and bruises they get at the hands of their husbands. You've never been married, Lancaster—"

"That's true, but if I was, I wouldn't beat my wife. That's just not right, Doc. I don't think a woman should put up with it."

The doctor laughed. "That makes you a rare man around here," he said. "I think it makes you a rare man this century."

"Well, maybe men won't be allowed to beat their wives in the next century."

Robert J. Randisi

"You and I will be long gone before that battle can be joined."

"Then we should fight the one we have in front of us now."

"Let me think about your proposal."

"You have less than two days," Lancaster said. "The judge is going to put a jury together tomorrow, and take Liz to court the day after."

"He is in a hurry to put her away," the doctor said.

"Yeah, he is," Lancaster said, "and then probably me, and I'm not going to let him do either."

Chapter Fifty-one

Next Lancaster went to the jailhouse to make sure Liz was still safe.

"No repeat of last night," Jessup told him. "I think we managed to convince them not to come back. You want to go and see your girl?"

"She's not my—"

"Just go and see her."

Liz was sitting on her bunk, staring into space when Lancaster entered the cellblock.

"Hello, Lancaster," she said with a wan smile. "You don't look like a happy man."

"I can't say I am," he said. He told her about his visit to the whorehouse in Tateville.

"Well," she said, "I wouldn't expect those women to care enough about me to come here and risk their lives by going against the judge. Why would they?"

"I just thought you'd have something in common and they might want to help."

"Did Mike tell you that we have a court date?"

"Yes," Lancaster said. "I wonder if the judge will have any women on the jury."

"I think you've already discovered that it might not be so helpful to us even if he did."

"People seem to think I should take care of the judge the same way I took care of three of his sons."

"Just kill him?"

"You'd be safe if I did that," Lancaster said. "You'd probably still stand trial, but at least you'd have a different judge."

"You can't do that, Lancaster," she said. "You had no choice with Ben and the others, but this would be murder."

"I know that."

"You've got to do something else."

"Well, I still don't think you killed Harry," he said. "Tell me who else might have wanted to?"

She lowered her head. "I can't."

"Why not?"

"I can't just name somebody to get myself out of trouble."

"I just need a suggestion, Liz," Lancaster said. "Something I can follow up. Somebody killed your husband, and I'd like to find out who did it. That'd be the easiest way to get you off."

She put her head in her hands and shook it. "Harry was not a nice man, Lancaster," she said. "A lot of people probably wanted to kill him. I wouldn't put it past any of his brothers."

"And his father?"

"The judge would do anything," she said. "There's no limit to his . . . evil! My God, the whole time I was married to Harry, why did I never think of that word? They were all evil, and now only the judge is left."

"Okay," Lancaster said, "then I need to talk to the undertaker."

"What for?"

"I want to get a look at the bottom of the dead men's boots," he said. "I'll talk to you tomorrow."

He left the cellblock and asked the sheriff, "Is it too late to get the undertaker to show me the boots the Burketts were wearing?"

"His name is Clyde Blackwood. He lives in the back, so just keep banging on the door until he answers it, and then tell him I sent you. He'll show you what you want."

"Thanks, Sheriff."

Another late-evening meeting between the judge and Vin Noble. The judge was standing with his hands clasped behind his back, looking out the window.

"This would all be over if that mob had achieved its goal last night," he said.

"That would've got rid of the girl, not Lancaster," Vin pointed out.

"Still . . . if you had been in with that mob . . ."

"I see, I could've killed Lancaster then," Vin said. "And I would've had to kill the sheriff."

"Small loss."

"Well, I can go over to the saloon tonight and incite them again, but three men died last night. They're not gonna forget that no matter how drunk they get."

Robert J. Randisi

"I know," the judge said. Then he turned and faced Vin. "All right, it was a missed opportunity. So we move on."

"You'll get your jury together tomorrow?"

"Twelve good and true people who will see the girl for what she was is—a murderer."

"You hope."

"I will make sure!"

"And once she's convicted?"

"Lancaster's only witness will be discredited," the judge said. "And so will he."

"And then I get 'im?"

"And then you can have him, my boy."

Chapter Fifty-two

Lancaster did just as the sheriff suggested—he pounded on the undertaker's door until the man answered it. He was in his thirties, disheveled, sleepy and did not seem to be someone who had been an undertaker for a very long time.

"What the blue blazes—" he started, but Lancaster cut him off.

"The sheriff sent me over," he said. "He wants you to show me the boots the Burkett boys were wearing when they were killed."

"Their boots?" the man asked, surprised.

"Yeah," Lancaster said. "You still have them, don't you? You didn't sell them yet?"

"Wha—what—"

"Oh, I know the racket," Lancaster said. "Tell the relatives of the deceased that they are buried with their boots on when you actually buried them in their socks. Then you sell the boots."

"Mister, I don't know what—"

"Look, I don't care if you sell the boots," Lancaster said. "I just want to see them. Do you still have them?"

"Well, y-yes—"

"Let me see them."

"Oh, all right! This way."

Lancaster followed him into a room where clothing was piled in a corner. Off to one side was a set of shelves with four sets of boots on them. Lancaster assumed they were from the four Burkett brothers.

"There," Blackwood said, pointing.

Lancaster walked to the shelves, lifted the sets of boots one at a time and examined the bottoms.

"Well?" Blackwood asked.

"No holes."

"Of course not," Blackwood said. "How would I be able to sell them if they had holes?"

Lancaster put back the boots. This was a dead end.

He could only think of one other way to proceed.

Vin Noble had found the little saloon where Hector Adams used to meet with Eddie Pratt to drink. Adams was off his feet, and Pratt was dead.

Vin was there with the two men he had brought into town for backup. Hoyt Dixon and Jed Carter were not gunman, but they were useful when it came to gunplay. Vin had used them as backup before and it had always worked. They were about the same age as each other, but ten years younger than he was, so they looked up to him as a mentor.

They didn't know it, but he looked at them as disposable.

Vin Noble bought a round of drinks and fielded questions.

"When do we go?" Dixon asked.

"When I say."

"And when is that?" Carter asked.

"When the man says," Vin replied.

"And who's the man?" Dixon asked.

"He's the man with the money."

Dixon and Carter did not know the actual relationship between the judge and Vin, and they did not know whom Vin was working for. All they knew was that they were working for Vin.

"The girl's going on trial soon," Vin said. "Once she's convicted, we'll know what we're gonna be doin'."

"And if she ain't convicted?" Dixon asked.

"Either way," Vin said, "this'll be over in about two days."

Lancaster entered the sheriff's office, surprising the lawman as he was pouring himself a cup of coffee.

"Back so soon?"

"Sheriff, I need to take Liz out of here."

"Lancaster, I can't let her out. I'd like to help you, but I can't just—"

He froze when Lancaster drew his gun. The sheriff was still holding the pot in one hand and the mug in his other.

"What the hell are you doin'?"

"Put the pot and mug down." Lancaster did not want to chance getting hot coffee in his face. "Now stand still and put your hands up." He stepped forward, plucked the sheriff's gun from his holster and tossed it aside.

"Lancaster, this isn't the way—"

"This is the only way. Into the cellblock."

In passing, Lancaster grabbed the key ring from a wall peg.

"Lancaster, what—" Liz started.

"We're getting out of here," he said, pushing the sheriff into a cell. He closed the door and locked it, then moved to Liz's cell and unlocked her door.

"Running is not the way to do this, Lancaster."

"Is that what we're doing, Lancaster?" Liz asked. "Running?"

"Not quite," he said.

Chapter Fifty-three

Lancaster and Liz rode double on his horse as they left town.

"Where are we going?" she asked.

"You'll see."

She wrapped her hands around his waist and pressed her face against his back. That kept her from seeing where they were going until it was too late.

Lancaster reined in his horse, felt Liz's grip on him lessen. He grabbed her hand and eased her down to her feet.

"Where are—" she started, but then she saw. They had ridden out to her house. "No."

"Yes," he said, dismounting.

They were back where it had all started. The only difference was that it was dark out now.

"We can't stay here, Lancaster," she said. "The sheriff will figure out where we are."

"He's in a cell."

"But . . . someone will let him out."

"It's late," he said, "he has no deputies and no one can hear him shouting from that cell."

"Lancaster—"

"Liz," he said, putting his hand on the small of her back, "going inside might bring it all back to you. Then we'll know."

"I-I'm not sure if I want to know."

"We have to know the truth, Liz," Lancaster said. "It's all we have left."

Liz hugged herself tightly, then said to Lancaster, "I have to go slow."

"That's okay," he said. "We'll go at your pace."

It took an hour before Liz finally got to the front door. Lancaster went inside and lit some lamps so that the interior of the house was bathed in a warm golden glow.

At the door, Liz looked inside.

"Anything?" Lancaster asked.

"N-no."

"Come inside the door."

Liz hesitated, then took a few steps.

"How do you feel?"

"Panicky."

Lancaster started straightening up the house, setting furniture back on its feet. He figured maybe if the place looked the way it did before everything happened, it might bring something back.

She was far enough inside for him to close the front door. What he'd said about the sheriff was true, but that didn't mean someone wouldn't come looking when they saw the lights.

Liz started a bit when he closed the door, but she didn't run.

"Do you want to sit?" he asked.

"Will you sit with me?"

"Of course," he said. "Let's sit on that sofa. It looks pretty comfortable."

"It is," she said. "I've sat there many nights, reading."

Lancaster walked with her to the sofa and they both sat down.

"Did you sit here with Harry?"

"No," she said. "Never."

Abruptly, she put her head on his shoulder. Within minutes she was asleep.

Lancaster wondered whether this was going to work at all.

Chapter Fifty-four

When Liz woke the lamps had gone out, but the early-morning sun was coming in through the windows. The house was lit up with daylight, as it had been that day. . . .

That day . . .

Harry had awakened angry, as he often did. He'd started berating her before breakfast, during breakfast and after breakfast, calling her a bitch, all kinds of other names, saying she wasn't good enough for him. She had made the mistake of telling him that maybe a baby would save their marriage. That only made him angrier. He had stood up so quickly that he knocked over the chair he'd been sitting in. He'd closed on her quickly and had savagely punched her in the stomach.

Lying on the floor, she saw him draw back his foot, as if he were planning to kick her. She thought she was going to die. But he didn't kick her. He'd walked over to the wall, where he hung his gun belt every night, and drew the gun from its holster. Also on the wall was a rifle, and Liz knew he kept a shotgun in the bedroom, in case someone tried to break in at night.

She scrambled to the bedroom, not even trying to get to her feet. She crawled into the room and reached under the bed, pulled out the shotgun, hoping it was loaded.

Harry came rushing into the room, roaring, waving his gun . . . and . . . and there was someone else in the room. . . .

"He hit me again," she said to Lancaster, as she related the story to him. "Pushed me down, pulled the shotgun away from me."

"So at this point you don't have the shotgun in your hands anymore?"

"No."

"And who was the other person in the room?"

"I don't know," she said. "A man—I know that. After Harry knocked me down the man moved. He—he must've hit Harry, and pulled the shotgun away from him. Harry staggered back and . . . I heard the shot. There was a wet sound, blood was everywhere, and Harry was on the floor."

"And the other man?"

"Gone," she said. "Out the window, I think."

"And what did you do?"

"I crawled to Harry to see if he was alive. I—I grabbed him, shook him, got his blood all over me . . . and then his brothers came running in. They said they'd heard the shot . . . and then they stopped when they saw Harry. After that it gets even . . . fuzzier. They hit me a few times, I know, then dragged me outside . . . and that's when you came."

They were still seated on the sofa, but she had scooted back, so they were sitting at opposite ends.

"So you never pulled the trigger on the shotgun?"

"No," she said. "I didn't. I remember now, Lancaster. I didn't!"

"You didn't kill your husband, Liz."

"No, I didn't," she said happily—and then, just as quickly, the happiness was gone. "But how do we prove it?"

"We have to find the other man," he said, "which really puts us back where we were before."

"Except that the sheriff's got to be very angry with you," she said.

"I know," he said, "but if we can get to town soon and let him out, there's no chance he'll be embarrassed by what we did. Come on."

As he pulled her to her feet she said, "This was a good idea, Lancaster."

"Yes," he said, "it was, because at least now you know."

Chapter Fifty-five

They managed to return to the jail without incident. The town was waking up, but they came up on the building from behind. The back door was locked so Lancaster slipped around to the front and entered, went to the cellblocks to let Liz in the back.

"You sonofabitch, you lost her, didn't ya?" Jessup demanded as he went by his cell.

Lancaster didn't answer. He unlocked the back door and Liz slipped inside.

"Oh," Jessup said.

Lancaster fetched the cell key and let Jessup out.

"Sorry you had to spend the night in a cell, Sheriff," Lancaster said. "We had to return to the house to see if it would jog her memory."

"And did it?"

"Yes," Lancaster said, "she remembers what happened."

"Oh? Can she remember how to make a pot of coffee?" Jessup asked.

"You're not putting me back in a cell?" she asked.

"Not if you can make better coffee than I can."

"Well, since you've given me a cup or two of your coffee, I'm pretty sure I can."

"Let's go in the office and you can tell me what happened."

Liz made a pot of coffee that was far better than anything the sheriff had ever made, while Lancaster told the sheriff what had happened.

"So you didn't see the other man at all?" Jessup asked.

"I was on the floor," she said. "Harry had hit me in the face."

"But she remembers that she didn't pull the trigger, Sheriff," Lancaster said.

Jessup gave Lancaster a look. "If I believed every prisoner who said they didn't pull the trigger . . ."

"Well, then why haven't you put her back in a cell?" Lancaster asked.

"I was wondering if you'd try to stop me," Jessup said.

Lancaster looked at Liz.

"No," she said. "If he wants me to go back into a cell, I must."

"Then we're right back where we started," Lancaster said.

"But at least I know I didn't kill Harry," she said. "I'll just have to wait for you to prove it."

Jessup stood up.

"I have to put her back, Lancaster."

She put down her coffee cup. Jessup took her to a cell and Lancaster didn't try to stop him.

When Jessup reappeared Lancaster had poured himself another cup of coffee.

"Don't think I'll ever drink my own again," he said, sitting at his desk. He grabbed his cup, then put his feet on his desk. Lancaster remembered seeing the man in that position before, but he hadn't noticed then what he noticed now: a hole in the right boot, right where the ball of the foot was. And to go along with it, a worn-down heel.

Chapter Fifty-six

Lancaster had two thoughts.

Walk over to the desk and knock the sheriff's feet off.

Stow this information away for later.

"What's on your mind?" the lawman asked. "You look like you saw a ghost."

"Hmm? Oh, nothing. I'm just thinking. I've got to go and see Delaney, see what he has to say."

"Sure, you do that."

"Look, I'm sorry about putting you in one of your own cells."

"I should lock you up for breakin' her out," Jessup said, "but I ain't gonna."

"Thanks."

"The judge should be gettin' his jury together today."

"How does he usually do that?"

"He picks 'em," Jessup said. "He knows who he likes for his juries, and nobody ever tells him no. One thing might be different, though."

"What's that?"

"He usually uses his boys to bring the people in," the sheriff said. He shrugged. "I don't know what he'll do now."

In the Judge's office, Vin Noble said, "You want me to do what?"

"I want you to go with my clerk and pick up my jury," the judge said.

"If I do that," Vin said, "everybody in town is going to know I'm working for you."

"I realize that," the judge said. "and at this point in time, I don't care."

"But . . . I don't know these people," Vin went on. "I don't know where to find them."

"That's why Simon will be going with you," the judge said. "He'll show you where they are and you will tell them I want them."

"What if they say no?"

"You," the judge said, "will make it very clear that *no* is not an option."

Lancaster left the sheriff's office, remembering that Mike Delaney had told him not to trust anyone, even the lawyer himself. There was a time in Lancaster's life when no one would have had to tell him that. Even though he had been a killer back then, there were many aspects of that life he missed. One was that he had been sharp all the time. Over these past few years, though, he felt he had gotten lazy. A lot of that was due to the time he'd spent in the bottle. As far as physical ability and mental sharpness, he had not yet come all the way back since he'd left the bottle behind.

He went back to his hotel, for want of anyplace else to go. He wasn't ready yet to tell Delaney that he had found the owner of the boot with the hole in it. The only thing he was a hundred percent sure of was that it had been the sheriff who had tried to take a shot at him in his cell. Once he'd snatched the gun away, the lawman had probably quickly run around to the front of the jail so he could come running into the cellblock as if he'd just heard the shot. The whiskey smell, that must have been a plant just in case, so that Lancaster would think some drunk had gotten brave.

The boot print under the window of the Burkett house meant the sheriff had been there, but he couldn't be even ninety percent sure that the sheriff had killed Harry, his own deputy. However, as of this moment he seemed more likely to have pulled the trigger than Liz did.

As her entered the hotel the desk clerk waved frantically at him. "A lady left you a message," the man said, holding it out.

"When was this?"

"Yesterday," the clerk answered. "She seemed very anxious to talk to you.'

"Do you know who she was?"

"Um, I think it says it in the note."

Lancaster unfolded the note. It read, *Come to my house as soon as you read this. It's very important*. It was signed, *Rusty Connors*.

Lancaster looked at the clerk, who looked away

nervously. At the bottom of the note Rusty had written her address.

"Can you tell me how to get to this address?" he asked the man.

"Uh, yes, of course, sir," the clerk said.

Chapter Fifty-seven

Following the clerk's directions led Lancaster to a part of town where he would not have expected to find Rusty Connors. From the little he'd learned about her, he'd have expected her to have a small cabin outside of town. But here she was in a lavish home in the better part of Gallows. He wondered how she was able to afford a home like this, but figured he might be about to find out.

He knocked on the door and Rusty Connors answered it. She looked like an unhappy woman, and the swelling and bruising under one eye was not the half of it.

"Finally," she said, with no relief at all. "I was looking for you yesterday."

"I was away overnight," he said. "I just got your message."

"Well, you better come in before somebody sees you," she said, backing away. She was dressed simply, as she had been the last time he'd seen her. It made it all the more odd she was living in this house.

"You live in this house?" he asked, looking around the large foyer.

"I have been," she said, "but not for much longer. Come with me. I was having a drink."

She led him into a sparsely furnished sitting room, walked across the room to a sideboard.

"I'm having a whiskey," she said, picking up a glass. "You?"

"No, thanks." He drank beer, but he didn't touch whiskey anymore.

"You're probably wonderin' why I asked you to come here, so I'll get right to the point," she said. "I can help you get the judge."

"How?"

"Have you talked to his wife?"

"Yes," Lancaster said. "She was helpful as she could be while talking to a man she hated."

"Did she mention he had a mistress?"

"Yeah, and somebody else mentioned it, as well. Now you'll be the third."

"Yes, but I can tell you who it is."

"Who?" he asked, and then, before she could reply, he asked, "You?"

"That's right," she said, "me. Until two nights ago."

"What happened two nights ago?"

"He did this," she said, pointing to her face.

"First time for you?" he asked.

"First," she said, "and last. Remember what I told you in Liz's hotel room?"

"You said if a husband hit you, you'd kill him."

"See, he ain't my husband," she said, "and I didn't kill him, but I'll help you get him."

"How?"

"You name it," she said. "You want me to testify for Liz, I will. Just tell me what to say."

"You'd perjure yourself?"

"Nobody would know it was perjury except the judge," she said, "and what could he do about it?"

Lancaster remembered what Delaney had said in reply to his question about the judge reversing a jury's decision. Even if Rusty's testimony got the jury to acquit Liz and the judge reversed it, though, he'd still have to explain his decision. The judge couldn't just come out and explain that he knew she was lying; he'd have to say how he knew.

"I appreciate the offer, Rusty," he said. "I'll tell her lawyer, and we'll probably take you up on it, but I still don't know how much good it will do."

"If you got other women to testify—"

"I tried that," he said, cutting her short. "I went to Tateville, but none of the women at the whorehouse there will testify."

"I'll bet there's somebody you haven't asked," she said.

"Who?"

"The judge's wife."

"She hates me," he said, "and I believe she's hated Liz the whole time she was married to Harry."

"Well, there's hate," she said, "and then there's *hate*."

"What do you mean?"

"Think about it," she told him. "Who do you think Mildred Burkett hates more than any other person alive?"

That would work, he thought, that would be the most damaging testimony they could get—the judge's wife testifying against the judge.

But could he get her to do it?

No, he probably couldn't. But there might be one or two people who could do it.

"Rusty," he said, "thanks very much. I'll be in touch."

"I'll only be here a couple of more days, maybe less," she said. "Once he knows I'm against him he'll throw me out."

"I'll try to get back to you before then," he said. "Stay safe."

"He won't do anything drastic."

Lancaster stopped before leaving and turned back.

"How long have you been . . . with him?"

"Months."

"Why?"

"Look around you," she said. "I got tired of living in houses with dirt floors."

"But . . . why did it take him all this time to get violent with you?"

"Truthfully? I think your coming to town had a lot to do with it. He won't let it show, but you're getting' to him."

"I'm sorry—"

"Don't be," she said, waving away his apology. "I knew it was only a matter of time. Men like him

231

can't keep that part of themselves hidden for very long."

"What will you do after it's all over?"

"Leave town, find another place," she said. "It's what I always do. Don't apologize again," she said, cutting him off. "At least this time I'll be leavin' after doin' the right thing. Now you go, make your arrangements. Let me know when and where you need me."

He almost said, "I'm sorry," again, but he replaced it with "thanks" and left.

Chapter Fifty-eight

"What makes you think she'd do it if I asked her?" Doctor Meade asked.

"You said you've known the judge a long time," Lancaster said. "I assumed that meant you knew Mrs. Burkett, too."

"You know I know her. I told you I've treated her."

"And I'll bet you've been a shoulder for her to cry on."

"What do you mean by that?" the doctor demanded.

They were alone in his office. This time Lancaster had found him doing paperwork, and not with a patient.

"I didn't mean anything more than I said, Doc," Lancaster said. "She had to talk to somebody about her problems. Why not her doctor?"

The doctor calmed down. "Well, yeah, she did talk to me, but she'd never take my advice about leavin' him."

"Maybe she's in a position to take your advice now, Doc."

"What else have you got?"

"The judge's mistress," Lancaster said. "She'll testify for Liz and against the judge."

"Rusty."

'You know her, too, huh?"

"Everybody in town has been my patient at one time or another, Lancaster," the doctor said.

"Will you ask her?"

"If I don't, who will?"

"I thought about having Mike Delaney ask."

"That wouldn't work," he said. "Mildred doesn't like him."

"Is there anybody in town Mildred likes?" Lancaster asked.

"Me," the doctor said, "so you see, you've come to the right person, after all."

"You'll get her to do it?"

"I'll ask her," Doc Meade said. "That's all I can do."

Lancaster went to Mike Delaney's office next, told him what he had so far. Except for the hole in the sheriff's boot. He was still keeping that to himself.

"So Rusty will testify that the judge hit her?" Delaney asked.

"Rusty will say anything we want her to," Lancaster said.

"Are you suggesting we have her perjure herself?"

"That's exactly what I'm suggesting."

"I can't do that, Lancaster," Delaney said. "I'm an officer of the court."

"I'm not saying we have her say she saw who killed Harry Burkett, Mike," Lancaster said. "I'm just saying we have her say some things about the judge. He can't refute them without admitting his relationship to her."

"There are a few people in town who already know about that, Lancaster."

"Some, maybe, but not all. And not people from other towns, other counties, from the state capital."

"I can't condone any kind of lying in court, Lancaster," Delaney said. "What else have you got?"

"The judge's wife," Lancaster said. "The doc's going to ask her if she'll testify."

"Why would she?"

"Because she hates him even more than she hates me."

"Well, that I can use," Delaney said. "But you'll have to figure out some other way to use Rusty."

"Why don't you just use her to say how violent the judge got with her?" Lancaster said. "It'll match what his wife says."

"I can do that," Delaney said, "but I don't know if it'll be enough. If we had some women to testify about the sons, about Harry, that would corroborate Liz's story. But even then I don't know if a jury will acquit a woman who killed her husband because he beat her."

"Why, because it's accepted?"

"Let's just say it happens a lot," Delaney said. "But saying that a woman was justified in killing her husband because he beat her up, that'd be like saying she could kill him for . . . well, raping her.

235

And how could a husband rape his own wife? He's got rights, doesn't he? As a husband?"

"Beating a wife," Lancaster said, "and raping her? You call those rights?"

"Everybody does," Delaney said helplessly. "Look, you're lucky you caught me here. I've got to get back to the courtroom for jury selection. It's not over. The judge and the prosecuting attorney are waiting."

"Prosecuting attorney? I haven't met him."

"There's been no need for you to," Delaney said, "and if you never do, it'll be better that way."

"Who's bringing his jury members in now that his boys are gone?"

"Some fella named Noble, Vincent Noble. I don't know who he is—wait a minute. That's the guy you said you thought the judge brought to town."

"I guess now we know it for sure," Lancaster said. "He works for the judge."

"I've got to go, Lancaster. Stay here as long as you want. Just pull the door shut when you leave."

After Delaney left Lancaster sat behind the lawyer's desk and thought about what he had. Suddenly he was in possession of more ammunition than before. Rusty Connors would testify for Liz, and the sheriff's boots were testifying, too. If only the doctor could get Mildred Burkett to agree to testify . . . Maybe he'd be able to use all of that even before they got to court.

Maybe Rusty and Mildred wouldn't even have to testify. Maybe he could just use their willingness to do it against the judge. And then once he proved that the sheriff, not Liz, had killed Harry, maybe the judge would see the folly in taking Liz into his courtroom.

He needed something else, though. Just one more thing might do it.

Chapter Fifty-nine

Lancaster went to court.

As he arrived he saw Vin Noble ahead of him, escorting a couple of people into the courtroom. He entered behind them, saw the people walk to the front, where the judge was waiting behind his bench. Noble had taken up a position in the back of the room. Lancaster stood next to him, leaning against the wall.

"Guess we know who hired you now," he said.

"Figured it would come out sooner or later."

"So, when are you supposed to take care of me?" Lancaster asked. "Before or after the trial?"

Noble looked at him and smiled. "I suppose whenever the judge says."

"What's wrong with right now?"

"You calling me out, Lancaster?"

"I don't do that sort of thing anymore, Noble," Lancaster said.

"No, that's right," Noble said, "you're a solid citizen."

"You've got backup in town, don't you?"

"What makes you say that?"

"That's the kind of man you are, Vincent," Lancaster said. "You'd never face me without backup."

Noble turned toward Lancaster, his face turning red. "I don't need any help taking care of you, Lancaster. You're through. You're all washed up. You've just been wandering around these past few years, waiting to die. Well, I'm gonna put your waiting to a stop."

"Not without help, you're not," Lancaster said, casually pushing away from the wall. "That's just not your style, Noble. You don't have the guts for it."

Lancaster walked away, out the door into the hall. In seconds Noble came through the door after him.

"Don't walk away from me!" he shouted.

"Why not?" Lancaster asked without turning. "I'm giving you my back, Vincent. Doesn't that make you comfortable?"

He heard Noble's gun clear leather and hoped he'd read the man right. The shot came and a piece of hot lead went flying past his ear.

"I could've had you then, Lancaster," Noble said, "but I want you to turn around."

Lancaster stopped and turned. At that moment the door to the courtroom opened and the judge came out.

"What the hell is going on out here?" he demanded.

"Hey, Judge," Lancaster said. "Your boy here took a shot at me and missed. At this range. Doesn't look like money well spent to me."

"What? I wasn't even trying to hit you, you sonofabitch. I should—" Noble pointed the gun at him.

"Vin, put that gun down!" the judge said.

"He's pushing me, Judge," Noble said. "And he ain't telling the truth."

Another man came out behind the judge—a slender man in his forties with his hair parted in the middle. Lancaster assumed it was the prosecutor. He was followed out by some of the would-be jurors, as well as Mike Delaney.

"Vincent. I'm telling you to put that gun down. Now is not the time or the place."

"Why not?" Noble demanded. "This is as good a time as any, Judge. You want him dead, he's gonna be dead."

Noble holstered his gun. "There you go, Lancaster. Fair and square. You and me."

"You're calling me out, Vincent?"

"Vin, boy, don't do it."

"Forget it, Daddy," Noble said. "You ain't telling me what to do anymore."

"Your backup's not here yet, Vin," Lancaster said, emulating the judge in calling him that. "You're not really going to try this without them, are you?"

"You sonofabitch!"

Noble went for his gun, a swift move that Lancaster recognized as being faster than he was. He drew his own gun deliberately, though, with no rush. The other man rushed his first shot and it went wide, creasing Lancaster's left arm, as it almost missed the mark completely. Lancaster fired once, hitting Noble right in the chest before the man could get off a second, deadlier shot. The gunman stepped back once, coughed, frowned, then dropped his gun and fell over onto his face.

The onlookers had scattered when the shooting started, but they had all been witness to it. They had all heard what was said.

The judge walked to the fallen man and looked down at him. Then he looked at Lancaster with no expression on his face.

"You think this will make a difference?" he asked, pointing downward. "You take my last son, and think it will change my mind?"

"I didn't know he was your son, Judge. I just thought he was your hired gun. But now everybody here knows he was both."

The judge turned his head and stared at the onlookers.

He stood rigid, didn't move, then looked back at Lancaster.

"Someone," he said without taking his eyes from Lancaster, "get the sheriff."

Chapter Sixty

When the sheriff arrived the judge said, "Take this man's gun and put him in a cell."

"What's the charge?" the sheriff asked.

"He killed this man." The judge pointed to the dead Vin Noble. "So it's murder."

"I killed him fair and square," Lancaster said. "Ask anyone here."

The sheriff looked at the group of onlookers. The prospective jurors and the prosecutor all turned and walked back into the courtroom, clearly declaring their allegiances.

"I saw it, Sheriff," Mike Delaney said. "It was a fair fight."

The sheriff looked at the judge.

"Take his gun, I said."

The sheriff looked at Lancaster.

"I'm afraid you'll have to take it this time, Sheriff," Lancaster said, looking down at his holstered gun. "I killed this man fair and square. I am not going to jail for that."

The sheriff studied him.

"Well," the judge said. "Go and get it."

"I ain't about to die for you, Judge," the lawman said. "You take it if you want it."

"Why, you lily-livered—" The judge stopped. It was the first sign of emotion Lancaster had seen from the man. The front he kept up was cracking.

"Turn in your badge, Jessup. You're through," the judge said.

"If he does that, Judge, you'll have no law in this town at all," Lancaster reminded the man. "There are no deputies to take his place."

"I'll find someone."

"Take you a while," Lancaster said. "Who knows what can happen to a town with no law?"

"This doesn't change anything," the judge said. "That woman goes on trial for murder tomorrow, and after she's convicted, you're next." He turned to Delaney. "We still have a jury to put together." Then he turned to the sheriff. "And you see to it that woman is in court at nine a.m. tomorrow morning."

"So I still have a job?"

"You still have a job," the judge said, then added, "for now."

He turned and marched back into his courtroom, followed by Delaney.

"What did this accomplish?" the sheriff asked, pointing to the dead man.

"Well, for one thing, I don't have to wait for Noble to make his move," Lancaster said. "For another, we found out that he was also the judge's son."

"Jesus," Jessup said, "you killed another one of his sons?"

"The last one, I hope."

The sheriff shook his head. "I better clean up this mess."

"Be careful," Lancaster said. "Noble had to have had at least two other men with him as backup."

"Yeah?" the sheriff asked. "Where were they when he needed them?"

Lancaster thought about confronting the man at that moment, but decided against it. Tomorrow would be soon enough.

Tomorrow everything would be resolved.

Chapter Sixty-one

Lancaster was waiting for Delaney at his office when the doctor showed up.

"Looking for Mike, Doc? Should be back from jury selection soon."

"Either one of you will do," Doc Meade said, taking off his hat.

"You talk to Mrs. Burkett?"

The doc nodded.

"She'll be in court tomorrow mornin'," he said.

"You convinced her?"

"Didn't have to," he said. "She agreed right out. Guess she's finally had enough."

"Thanks, Doc."

The doctor waved and said, "I'll see you both in court."

About an hour later Mike Delaney showed up.

"Didn't know you were waiting here," he said to Lancaster.

"Didn't know your desk chair was so comfortable."

Delaney stared at him and Lancaster said, "Oh," and got up.

As Delaney seated himself, Lancaster asked, "Jury all set?"

"Yep."

"Doc was here. Said Mrs. Burkett will testify. She'll be in court tomorrow."

"The judge wants you more than ever, Lancaster, after today," Delaney said. "I don't know if Mrs. Burkett and Rusty will be enough."

"Well," Lancaster said, "all he's got left are Noble's two backup guns, and I doubt they'd want to step up."

"He's still got his courtroom."

"He cracked today, Mike," Lancaster said. "I saw it. He's ready. He's had everything bottled up inside of him for so long that he's ready to explode."

"And when he does?"

"Everybody will know he's crazy."

"I hope you're right. You want to have supper?"

"Sure, but let's make a stop first."

"Where?"

"Rusty Connors'," Lancaster said. "I want to make sure she's all set for tomorrow."

After they made sure Rusty would show up, and then had supper, Lancaster went to the jailhouse to tell Liz what had happened.

The sheriff was sitting at his desk with his feet up on it. That hole was still there, and now it looked a mile wide to Lancaster. How had he missed it before? There was also a couple of trays on the table, covered by checkered napkins.

"Just want to tell Liz about today," he said. "She had her supper yet?"

"Just finished," the lawman said. "In fact, I was waiting on you so I could bring the trays back."

"You go ahead. I won't be breaking her out again."

The sheriff dropped his feet to the floor, grabbed his hat and the trays and left.

Lancaster walked into the cellblock, found Liz lying on her back. She didn't get up when she saw him.

"Are we all set for tomorrow?" she asked.

"We've got a few tricks up our sleeves," he said. "Want to hear?"

"No," she said, "I'd rather be surprised. The sheriff told me there was a shooting today, though."

"Yeah."

"I didn't know the judge had another son."

"Nobody did, I guess."

"Are you going to be in court, Lancaster?"

"I'll be there, Liz. By the way, I've got another little surprise for you."

"What's that?"

"I'll tell you that one tomorrow, too."

"I'm tired," she said. "So tired. I'm going to sleep good tonight. Might be my last chance to have a good night's sleep.'

"Don't give up yet, Liz."

"I thank you for all you've done since you first got here, Lancaster," she said. "Whatever happens,

247

I owe you a lot. You didn't have to take a hand in this at all. You could've just . . . kept riding."

"Actually," Lancaster said, "I don't think I ever really had a choice. Do you?"

Chapter Sixty-two

Lancaster was at the jail at eight thirty the next morning.

"Just in time," the sheriff said. "We finished breakfast and it's about time to go."

"Did she eat?"

"Like a horse," the lawman said. "Most appetite I've seen her have."

"Maybe that's a good sign."

"I think you're gonna need a lot more than that."

They both went back to the cells to get her. She smiled when she saw Lancaster.

"Thought I'd walk you over," he said. "Hope you don't mind."

"Not at all."

The sheriff opened the cell and she came out, linked her arm into Lancaster's.

"Ready?" Jessup asked.

"Ready as I'll ever be."

The three of them left the jail together and walked down to the courthouse. They had mounted the

Robert J. Randisi

boardwalk and were approaching the front door when suddenly there was some commotion down the street.

"What the hell?" Jessup asked, looking.

The sound reached them then, horses and a couple of wagons. People began to line the streets to watch, and when they came into view Lancaster saw that the two buckboards were loaded with women.

"What's going on?" Liz asked.

"I think I know," Lancaster said.

As the wagons got closer he could see that the women were wearing proper dresses and bonnets, but it was clear to him that these were two wagonloads of whores.

The wagons reached the courthouse and stopped. On the seat of the lead wagon was Maisie, from the whorehouse in Tateville.

"Mr. Lancaster. Sheriff."

"Maisie," the sheriff greeted, "what are you doin' here?"

"Well, after Mr. Lancaster left my place, I talked to my girls, and every one of them said they wanted to come and testify. Then I talked to the girls from the house in Garner, and they wanted to come, too. So here we are."

"All of 'em?" Jessup asked

"Every whore from both houses," Maisie said. "Them Burkett boys was mean."

Lancaster looked at Liz and smiled.

"Well," the sheriff said, "we better go inside."

* * *

250

Inside the courthouse, Lancaster and Jessup walked Liz up to the front, where Mike Delaney was waiting.

"What's going on outside?" Delaney said.

"All your witnesses have arrived."

"Huh?"

"You'll see."

"All rise," someone said, and the judge came out from behind the bench and sat down, dressed in his robes. At that moment the back doors opened and the whores came streaming in. The townspeople who had come for the trial and the jurors all stared and began to mutter. Across from Mike Delaney the prosecutor was watching with wide, watery eyes.

"Order!" the judge shouted. "There will be order in my court!" He banged his gavel. "What the hell is going on here?"

"My witnesses, Judge," Mike Delaney said. "They're all arriving."

"Witnesses?" the judge demanded. "Who are these women, Counselor?"

"Judge, these are all the, uh, employees of the, um, whorehouses in the towns of Tateville and Garner."

"Hi, Judge," one girl said, waving to him, and then another.

"This is an outrage!" the judge said. "What are they doing here?"

"They're going to testify, Judge," Delaney said, "about the way your sons treated women."

"Whores?" the judge demanded.

"Women, Judge," Lancaster said.

"And," a voice from the back said, "all women are not whores."

"Who said that?" the judge demanded.

"I did."

As the judge watched, his wife stood up in the back of the courthouse.

"Mildred, what the hell are you doing here?" he demanded.

"She's another one of my witnesses, Judge," Delaney said.

"Wha—"

"Oh, and here's another," Delaney said as the door opened again and Rusty Connors came walking in.

"All right," the judge said, "Mr. Delaney, what do you expect to accomplish by filling my courtroom with—"

"Women, Judge?" Delaney asked. Then he faced the jury. "Ladies and gentlemen, what I intend to prove is that Harry Burkett—and, in fact, all the Burkett men—knew only one way to treat women, and that was to beat them."

Lancaster could see the judge's face turning red. One more crack in the man's veneer.

"My sons—" the judge started, but Mildred Burkett cut him off from the back of the room.

"Learned from their father how to brutalize women," she shouted. "And that is what got them killed, you bastard!"

"Ladies and gentlemen," Delaney said to the jury, "this goes beyond a husband beating a wife.

This is about men and women, and just how much a woman is expected to take."

"Stop that!" the Judge shouted, banging his gavel. "Stop talking to the jury. This trial has not begun yet."

"Then let's get started, Judge," Lancaster said. "That's what we're all here for, isn't it?"

The Judge glared at Lancaster, his face growing redder. He stood there with his gavel in his hand, and Lancaster thought that if the wooden hammer were a gun, he'd be dead by now.

And then there *was* a gun in the judge's hand, a silver revolver that he produced from somewhere beneath his robes. He started to bring it to bear, then hesitated, as if he didn't know who he wanted to shoot first, Lancaster, Delaney or his wife.

Everyone in the courtroom gasped and ducked except Lancaster, who stood up and drew his gun, but before he could fire—and before the judge could fire—the robed man suddenly sat down in his chair, his chin on his chest. As everyone looked on they heard his gun hit the floor.

"Judge?" Sheriff Jessup said.

"Judge?" Delaney asked.

"Doc?" Lancaster called. "Is Doc Meade here?"

"I'm here," the old doctor said, coming down the aisle. "Move aside."

The doctor made his way to the bench and examined the judge.

"He's dead," he announced. "It looks like a heart attack."

"Dead?" Mildred Jessup said. "That miserable bastard can't just die! He has to pay."

Lancaster approached the bench. "Can he just . . . die like that, Doc?"

"He did, Lancaster," the doc said. "He just did."

"So now what do we do?" Jessup asked. "We're all here for a trial, and we got no judge."

"We don't have a sheriff, either," Lancaster said, drawing his gun and pointing it at Jessup.

"What are you doin', Lancaster?" Jessup demanded. "This ain't funny."

"Take your gun out and drop it on the floor . . . now!" Lancaster said.

"Wha—"

"Do it!"

Jessup took out his gun and dropped it.

"Kick it away."

He did.

"Now, Jessup," Lancaster said, "in front of all these people, we're going to talk about boots . . . and murder."

Chapter Sixty-three

"Easiest case I ever won," Mike Delaney said.

"You were wonderful," Liz Burkett told him.

It was later in the day and they were all at the jailhouse. Ex-sheriff Jessup was in a cell.

"Who would've known that Jessup and Harry Burkett were partners?" Delaney said.

"They were buying up property in town," Lancaster said, "without his brothers knowing, and without the judge knowing."

"I didn't even know," Liz said.

"Harry was gettin' ready to take on his father," Doc Meade said. "Show him what kind of man he'd turned into."

"Only the sheriff didn't agree with his plans," Lancaster said. "So he went out to the house to kill Harry, and walked in on a fight between husband and wife."

"And used it to his advantage," Delaney said. "Kill Harry, blame it on Liz."

"B-but . . . what about the other three?" Liz asked. "How did they get there?"

She looked around at all the men in the room.

Finally, Doc said, "Coincidence?"

"They just happened to stop by?" Delaney asked.

"We'll never know," Lancaster said.

"So what does this all mean?" Liz asked. "Will you get another judge? Will I still have to go on trial?"

"No, my dear," Doc Meade said, "but Jessup will. You're free to go."

"Doesn't that take a judge, or at least a sheriff to say?" Delaney asked.

"Well," Doc said, "we can make it legal."

He picked Jessup's sheriff's star up from the desk and pinned it on Lancaster.

"Wha—" Lancaster started.

"Didn't I ever tell you I'm the president of the town council?" Doc asked. "I can do this."

"What about the mayor?" Lancaster asked.

"The judge always said the town didn't need one with him here," Doc said.

"But I don't want to be sheriff, Doc. I want to leave," Lancaster said.

"Well, we need someone to release Liz, someone to take statements from all the witnesses today and someone to keep Jessup in a cell."

"Then get somebody else."

"Why not just wear it until we do?" Doc Meade asked.

"Yes, Lancaster," Liz said, sliding her arms around his waist, "after all you've done for me, there's no one else I would rather have set me free."

With all of them staring at him, Lancaster knew he was faced with another situation where he didn't have a choice.

"All right," he agreed, "but just until you find someone else, Doc."

"I'll start lookin' right away," the doctor said, "tomorrow . . . or the next day. . . . Maybe next week . . ."

The Classic Film Collection

The Searchers by Alan LeMay

Hailed as one of the greatest American films, *The Searchers*, directed by John Ford and starring John Wayne, has had a direct influence on the works of Martin Scorsese, Steven Spielberg, and many others. Its gorgeous cinematic scope and deeply nuanced characters have proven timeless. And now available for the first time in decades is the powerful novel that inspired this iconic movie.

Destry Rides Again by Max Brand

Made in 1939, the Golden Year of Hollywood, *Destry Rides Again* helped launch Jimmy Stewart's career and made Marlene Dietrich an American icon. Now available for the first time in decades is the novel that inspired this much-loved movie.

The Man from Laramie by T. T. Flynn

In its original publication, *The Man from Laramie* had more than half a million copies in print. Shortly thereafter, it became one of the most recognized of the Anthony Mann/Jimmy Stewart collaborations, known for darker films with morally complex characters. Now the novel upon which this classic movie was based is once again available—for the first time in more than fifty years.

The Unforgiven by Alan LeMay

In this epic American novel, which served as the basis for the classic film directed by John Huston and starring Burt Lancaster and Audrey Hepburn, a family is torn apart when an old enemy starts a vicious rumor that sets the range aflame. Don't miss the powerful novel that inspired the film the *Motion Picture Herald* calls "an absorbing and compelling drama of epic proportions."

To order a book or to request a catalog call:
1-800-481-9191
Books are also available at your local bookstore, or you can check out our Web site **www.dorchesterpub.com**.

"Conley is among the most productive
and inventive of modern Western novelists."
—Dale L. Walker, *Rocky Mountain News*

BARJACK AND THE
UNWELCOME GHOST

Marshal Barjack likes to keep peace and quiet in the tiny
town of Asininity. It's better for business at the Hooch
House, the saloon that Barjack owns. But peace and quiet got mighty hard to come by once Harm Cody came
to town. Cody's made a lot of enemies over the years and
some of them are hot on his trail, aiming to kill him—
including a Cherokee named Miller and a pretty little
sharpshooter named Polly Pistol. And when the Asininity bank gets robbed, well, now Cody has a whole new
bunch of enemies . . . including Barjack.

Robert J. Conley

"One of the most underrated and overlooked writers
of our time, as well as the most skilled."
—Don Coldsmith, Author of the Spanish Bit Saga

ISBN 13: 978-0-8439-6225-3

KENT CONWELL

"A great read. Be prepared for adventure."
—*Roundup* on *Chimney of Gold*

As the moon rises, the night riders come out, sweeping over ranches in the valley, bringing fear and intimidation. Someone wants the owners to sell—badly—but like a few other holdouts, Ben Elliott has sworn not to give up his land for any price. So the night riders have upped the stakes. Once they were content to rustle cattle, but now they've moved up to killing livestock…and murdering men. There's only so much a decent man can take. Ben Elliott has reached that point. It's time for him to fight back. It's time for the nights of terror to become…

Days of Vengeance

ISBN 13: 978-0-8439-6226-0

Based on the immortal hero from the bestselling
Riders of the Purple Sage!

ZANE GREY'S™ LASSITER

BROTHER GUN

JACK SLADE

Lassiter, the solitary hero from Zane Grey's *Riders of the Purple Sage*, became one of the greatest Western legends of all time. Now America's favorite roughrider is back in further adventures filled with gun-slinging action and rawhide-tough characters.

BLOOD BROTHER

Lassiter owed Miguel Aleman for saving his life. To repay the favor, he swears to protect Miguel's troublesome son Juanito. He never thought he'd have to make good on his oath so soon, though. When Juanito kills a horse trader in a drunken brawl, he faces the gallows—unless Lassiter can save him. But the only option Lassiter has is to break the law himself...which might very well leave him swinging right along with his blood brother.

ISBN 13: 978-0-8439-6238-3

INTERACT WITH DORCHESTER ONLINE!

Want to learn more about your favorite books and authors?
Want to talk with other readers that like to read the same books as you?
Want to see up-to-the-minute Dorchester news?

VISIT DORCHESTER AT:
DorchesterPub.com
Twitter.com/DorchesterPub
Facebook.com (Search Pages)

DISCUSS DORCHESTER'S NOVELS AT:
Dorchester Forums at DorchesterPub.com
GoodReads.com
LibraryThing.com
Myspace.com/books
Shelfari.com
WeRead.com